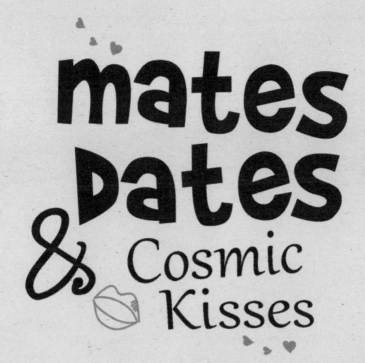

mates
Dates
& Cosmic
Kisses

Piccadilly

**Cathy Hopkins** lives in Bath with her husband and boisterous cats. She has had over sixty books published in thirty-four languages, and especially loves to write for teens. She is best known for the incredibly successful *Mates, Dates* series, let alone the *Truth, Dare and Cinnamon Girl* books, and also the *Zodiac Girl* and *Million Dollar Mates* series.

In her spare time, Cathy loves nothing more than a long walk followed by a pub lunch in the countryside with friends. She loves reading books from all types of genres and when wit's raining she likes to relax watching great DVD boxsets.

# mates Dates & Cosmic Kisses

Cathy Hopkins

*Thanks to my husband, Steve Lovering, without whom
my life would have no meaning. (He told me to write that but
I do mean the thanks bit. Honest.) And thanks to Brenda and
Jude at Piccadilly for their input and for giving me an excuse to watch
Dawson's Creek in the name of research. And lastly to Rosemary
Bromley, for all her encouragement and being a pal.*

First published in Great Britain in 2001
by Piccadilly Press,
A Templar/Bonnier publishing company
Deepdene Lodge, Deepdene Avenue,
Dorking, Surrey, RH5 4AT
www.piccadillypress.co.uk

Text copyright © Cathy Hopkins, 2001, 2007, 2014

A catalogue record for this book is available from
the British Library

ISBN: 978 1 84812 367 0

1 3 5 7 9 10 8 6 4 2

Printed in the UK by CPI Group (UK) Ltd, Croydon, CR0 4YY

# Chapter 1

# The Bridesmaid of Frankenstein

Lucy's jaw dropped when I came out of the bathroom.

'Izzie! What on *earth* have you done?' she cried.

'It's different,' said Nesta.

Both of them stared at me like I'd stepped out of a horror movie.

'Do you like it?' I asked, giving them a twirl.

It was the day of the wedding of my boring stepsister Amelia to the equally boring Jeremy and I had to be bridesmaid with my other stepsister Claudia. Typically, Amelia chose a disgusting dress for me. Emerald green satin. Empire line. Awful.

But then I'd had an idea.

'I had to do something,' I said. 'I looked like I had a starring role in a Jane Austen costume drama.'

'Yes,' said Nesta, still gawping, 'but *green* hair?'

1

'It matches perfectly,' I grinned. 'Don't you like it?'

'I think it looks fab,' said Lucy. 'But what about school? Mrs Allen will kill you.'

'Oh it washes out after a week. It's only mousse. But I'm not going to tell Mum that.'

I looked at my reflection in my bedroom mirror. 'I like it and I think I might keep it in until Monday at least.'

'Won't your mum make you wash it out?' asked Nesta.

'She's been dashing about all morning and the car will be here any minute so by the time she sees me, it'll be too late.'

Lucy giggled. 'You look like an Irish colleen. All that emerald makes your eyes look even greener than normal.'

'Then my grandma would have been proud – Irish roots and all that. Geddit? Emerald green roots?'

They were staring at me as if I'd gone mad.

'*Hair* roots, dummies.'

'More like she'll turn in her grave,' said Nesta. 'I don't think wearing green stretched as far as hair.'

'Maybe her ghost will show up at the wedding,' I said, 'and when they get to that part where the priest says, "Anyone here got any objection?" her ghost will rise up to the ceiling groaning, yes I do, I *do*. My granddaughter has dyed her lovely long brown hair green.'

Lucy and Nesta laughed.

'Seriously though,' I continued, 'I wish you two were

coming. It's not fair. Everyone else was allowed to bring friends, at least to the reception. But then, I suppose because they're all grown up it's one rule for them, another for us.'

'Well, there might be some decent boys there,' said Nesta. 'You can practise my flirting tips.'

'Fat chance. It'll be deadly dull. There's not even a dance. Jeremy's an accountant and, like Amelia, is from a family of accountants. They even had the wedding cake made into the shape of a calculator.'

'What's her dress like?' asked Lucy, interested as always in the styles of things. She's thinking about going to Art college and being a dress designer when she leaves school.

'Big meringue. Makes her look enormous even though she's skinny. In fact, I don't know how she'll fit into the wedding car.'

'If I got married,' said Nesta, lying back on the cushions like Cleopatra, 'I'd look fantabulous. Of course, I'll be famous by then and there will be lots of press there as all the mags will want to buy the wedding photos.'

'What would you wear?' asked Lucy.

'Something slinky. Figure-hugging. Maybe ivory silk with no back. And I'd have my hair loose, like it is now, right down to my waist. Not stuck up in one of those awful styles a lot of women choose for their wedding day, you know, beehives, all stuck up on top. And I'd just carry a simple bouquet, a couple of lilies or something. Elegant. And I'll have the ceremony in the grounds of my mansion and there'll be loads of rock stars and celebrities there.'

'You'd look stunning whatever you wore,' I said, looking at her stretched out on my bed. Nesta's easily the best-looking girl in our class, if not our school. She's half-Jamaican and half-Italian and has drop-dead gorgissimo looks. She could be a model if she wanted but lately has decided that she'd prefer to be an actress instead.

Lucy's pretty too but in a different way to Nesta. She's petite with spiky blonde hair, and looked like an elf, sitting cross-legged in her favourite place on the beanbag on my floor.

'What would you wear, Lucy?' I asked.

Lucy looked out of the window dreamily. 'I think I'd like to get married in winter, in the snow. In velvet, with a cloak. And little white rosebuds in my hair. I'd arrive at the church in a horse-drawn carriage and the church would be covered in flowers and ivy . . . '

'You're such a romantic, Luce,' I laughed. 'As long as you don't subject your bridesmaids to anything like this awful monstrosity I have to wear.'

'We would be the bridesmaids, wouldn't we?' asked Nesta. 'Being your best mates an' all?'

'Course, but I'd like to have Ben and Jerry as well, as they are my other best friends,' said Lucy.

'What?' exclaimed Nesta. 'Dogs at a wedding?'

'Yeah, they could be page-boys.'

Nesta and I had to hold our sides laughing. The idea of two fat Labradors waddling up the aisle with flowers round their necks was too much.

'Well I'm never getting married,' I said. 'What's the point? So many people split up a couple of years later. Like my mum and dad. Once, I overheard my dad on the phone saying he thought divorce was nature's way of saying "I told you so".'

'But you might fall in love one day,' said Lucy. 'And then you'll feel differently.'

'Nah. Look, I'm already fourteen and still not had a proper boyfriend. I've never met anyone who's come even close to what I want.'

'But if you did?' insisted Lucy.

'OK. If I did. Which I *won't*. I'd wear a red rubber mini-dress and roller-skate up the aisle with an all-singing all-dancing gospel choir in the background.'

'But I can't roller-skate,' said Lucy. 'And I have to be one of the bridesmaids.'

'Don't worry. It's not going to happen. I can't see me ever falling in love. Especially not if I stay round here. All the boys round here are total idiots.'

'Well I wouldn't want to get married for ages,' said Nesta. 'I want to play the field for as long as possible. Why settle for one fruit when you can try the whole basket?'

'You're such a tart,' said Lucy. 'Anyway, it's easy for you, being the boy magnet of North London. But what if you meet someone really special?'

'What, like Tony?' teased Nesta.

Poor Lucy went bright red. Tony is Nesta's older brother and Lucy has an almighty crush on him.

'He's asked me out on a date next week,' said Lucy shyly.

Nesta looked concerned. 'And are you going to go?'

'Course. But I know, I know, don't get too serious. I know what he's like. A different girl every week.'

'Don't you forget it,' warned Nesta. 'It's me and Iz who'd have to pick up the pieces.'

'I can look after myself,' said Lucy. 'But what about you, Iz? What do you want in a boy?'

'How long have you got?' I asked. 'Can I ask the audience? Go fifty-fifty? Phone a friend?'

'Final answer,' said Nesta. 'Give us your final answer.'

I had to think about this. The perfect boy?

'OK. Good sense of humour. Has to be able to make me laugh. Er, intelligent. I don't want some thick idiot. Someone I can talk to and have lots in common with.'

'Good-looking, surely?' asked Nesta.

'Yeah. A bit. I mean, I don't want a pin-up as I think a lot of boys that are way handsome are too cocky . . .'

'Like Tony,' said Nesta, looking pointedly at Lucy who ignored her.

'Er, excuse me,' I interrupted. 'I haven't finished. Final answer for the million dollar boy. GSOH. Intelligent. Generous. Decent looks. A nice bum. Genuinely likes girls' company. Clean fingernails and last but not least. . .'

'Rich,' said Nesta.

'Cute,' said Lucy.

'No,' I said, 'last but not least . . . able to stand on his head and sing "God Save the Queen".'

Lucy cracked up. 'You're mad, Izzie.'

'Good luck to you,' said Nesta. 'I mean, most of it sounds OK but *clean* fingernails? I think you're pushing it, girl.'

'Izzie,' called Mum frantically from downstairs. 'The car's here.'

I took a deep breath. 'Here I go! So. Final final question. Do I look all right? Green and all. Do you think I need more kohl on my eyes?'

'You look great,' said Lucy. 'And let us know how it all goes.'

'OK, Nesta?' I asked.

Nesta laughed. 'Well put it like this. When Amelia sees you, let's hope love really is blind.'

'If love is blind,' I said, 'then marriage will be an eye-opener.'

'Yeah, right,' said Nesta, getting up off my bed and heading for the door. 'Come on, Luce, I suggest we get out before Mrs Foster sees her and all hell breaks loose.'

Lucy grinned. 'Yeah. Nice knowing ya, Izzie.'

And with that, the two of them ran for it.

So much for my plan to freak out our headmistress with my green hair on Monday. As soon as we got back from the wedding, Mum marched me upstairs and into the bathroom.

'Right,' she said through gritted teeth. 'Start scrubbing and don't stop until your hair is back to normal.'

She handed me the shampoo and I waited for her to leave but she stood there glaring at me.

'It's not enough that you shame me in front of all our family and friends,' she continued, 'but you ruined Amelia's special day. And *how* are we going to explain the fact that one of the bridesmaids is missing from most of the wedding photographs?'

'I wouldn't have minded being in the pictures,' I began.

'Well Amelia minded. She was furious. Honestly, Isobel, fancy upstaging the bride on her wedding day.'

'I didn't mean to . . .'

'You never think, do you? You'd have stood out a mile in every photograph.'

'Sorry,' I said for the millionth time that day.

'And I won't have you going into school looking like that either. Lord knows what the teachers would think of us and what kind of home you come from.'

I was going to tell her loads of girls have coloured hair

and highlights but I know defeat when I see it so I bent over the taps and began washing.

Mum was still hovering as streams of green dye filled the bath. I could hear her sighing above the gushing water. I decided silence was the best policy so continued washing then reached for a towel.

'NOT THAT ONE!' cried Mum. 'For heaven's sake, Isobel!' (She always calls me by my full name when she's mad at me.) 'Not a white towel, it'll leave stains. I'll get you a dark one.'

Mum's very big on white towels. Once, after I'd been washing my face, she came into my room holding the towel I'd used.

'Is it you who's marked my towel?' she asked, pointing to mascara blotches. 'Towels are for drying with, not for using to remove make-up.'

Honestly. I wish she'd get some normal-coloured ones so I could use the bathroom without worrying, but then she's like that about everything. Our house is immaculate. Mum's immaculate. Always dressed in neat black suits for work and neat black trousers and cashmere sweaters for home. Dark hair in a neat bob. I don't know how she does it. Never a hair out of place. Never a scuff on her shoes. Never a mark on her clothing. Her star sign is Virgo, the perfectionist. She even cleans up before the cleaner comes in as she doesn't want her thinking we're a dirty family. What *is* the point of having a cleaner if you can't make a mess to clean up?

I wished she'd go away and let me finish doing my hair in peace but no, she plonked herself on the side of the bath and looked at me sternly. 'Now are you going to give me some kind of explanation?'

'Er, I . . . I thought it looked nice.'

Sigh. Bigger sigh.

'I didn't mean to upset anyone . . . ' I began.

I didn't. But I did get quite a reaction. We were going up the aisle and everyone was oohing and aahing at the bride when suddenly the guests all spotted me and the place went quiet. Then people looked away. But not Amelia. I could see the moment I caught her eye that there was going to be trouble. Big trouble. I swear I could see steam coming out from under her veil. I kept my eyes on the altar and prayed she'd mellow out a bit at the reception after a few drinks. She didn't. She went completely ballistic.

Mum was still glaring at me from the side of the bath. I didn't know what else to say.

'Um, sorry,' I said. 'Sorry, sorry.'

'Sorry? You don't know the meaning of the word. Go to your room. I can't bear to look at you.'

I crept into my room. Definitely in the doghouse. Definitely *persona non grata*. Again.

# Chapter 2

# A Strange-looking Parasite

'And where do you think you're going?' asked Mum the next day as I tried to sneak out the front door. I was hoping to escape before I was grounded.

'Out with Nesta and Lucy.'

'Have you had breakfast?'

'Not hungry,' I said, stuffing my gloves in my coat pocket.

'It's cold and raining out there. You can't go out without anything inside you. Come back.'

I followed her back into the kitchen and she started putting bread in the toaster.

'Er, no thanks, Mum, I'll just have some fruit. I don't eat white bread any more.'

'Since when?'

'Since now.'

'And why's that?' she asked. She was looking quite

cheerful considering the events of the day before. Was I forgiven?

'Er, no reason. I just don't fancy any.'

'Then I'll do you some eggs.'

'No thanks, I don't fancy eggs. I'll take some fruit.'

How can I tell her I only eat free-range now? I read how they keep the battery hens all cooped up in tiny spaces. Awful, poor little chicks. But I don't want to go there with Mum today, it would only start an argument.

'Izzie, what is it with you lately? Can't eat this, won't eat that!'

I took a deep breath. 'Well, see, we did a class on nutrition at school and I was wondering if, er, maybe we could have more healthy food.'

'What do you mean, more healthy food?'

'Like maybe fresh food rather than frozen, free-range eggs, maybe organic . . .'

'And what's wrong with what I give you?'

'Er, nothing wrong with it but we could be eating better.'

'Nonsense. We eat very well here. There's always plenty of food in the cupboards.'

'But Mum . . . I'm not talking about quantity, I'm talking about quality . . .'

'Are you saying my food isn't good quality?'

'No, NO . . .'

This wasn't going well.

I decided to try another angle. 'You know how you like everything to be immaculate in the house?'

'Yes.'

'Well, see, that's all external. What I'm talking about is what's inside. You are what you eat and the more fresh and healthy the food is that you eat, the better you feel and the more immaculate you are on the inside. You'd like that, wouldn't you?'

It was worth a try. She seemed to be considering what I'd said.

My stepfather Angus looked up over his *Financial Times*. 'What Izzie's saying is she wants to go green!'

Very funny. Not.

Thanks, Angus, I thought, last thing I need is someone reminding Mum of yesterday.

'No. Not green. I'm not talking about the environment. Although that's important too. I'm talking about not eating rubbish.'

Oops. Me and my big mouth. Didn't mean it to come out like that. Mum's stern expression returned in a flash.

'Why can't you be like normal teenagers, Izzie? Most girls your age want nothing but pasta and chips. Why do you always have to be different?'

'You can get organic pasta. Lucy's mum and dad buy all organic food. In fact, Mr Lovering sells it at his shop.'

'Well they're welcome to it. We don't live like them.'

Wish I did, I thought. Lucy's house is so different to mine. It's lived-in, cosy. *And* they have coloured towels in their bathroom so you can get them as dirty as you like.

'But Mum . . . it's a well-known fact that fresh produce is better for you than all that stuff you eat. Out of the freezer and into the microwave, full of preservatives . . . '

'Don't speak to your mother like that,' said Angus.

I can't win. I wasn't speaking to Mum like *that*. I thought we'd all benefit from my health suggestions but I'd wanted to pick my time for bringing it up. Escape seemed the best plan.

'Can I go now?' I asked, getting up.

'Not before you eat that toast,' said Mum.

'Whatever. I'll take it with me. I'll eat it. Promise.'

I wrapped the toast in a napkin and made a dash for the door. I'll feed it to the birds, I thought.

But I bet even they prefer wholemeal.


Lucy and Nesta were waiting for me at Camden tube station, standing by the ticket machines, munching on Snickers bars.

'We match,' I said, seeing we were all dressed in black.

'When in Camden,' said Nesta, 'do as the Camdens do . . . or something like that.'

Everyone in Camden seems to wear black or grey. Maybe it's to fit in with the December weather which as usual is dull and rainy.

'So how was the wedding?' asked Nesta as we fought our

14

way through the Sunday crowds to the indoor market at the Lock. 'I see your hair's back to normal.'

'I know. Mum went ballistic and made me wash the green out as soon as we got home. Amelia was furious when she saw me. She banned me from most of the wedding photos and said she'll never speak to me again.'

'Good result, then,' grinned Nesta. 'She was never your favourite person, was she?'

'Not really,' I laughed. 'And I don't think I ruined the day as much as everyone made out. The wedding was quite sweet in the end. Specially when one of the page-boys read out The Lord's Prayer. He was so cute, only six. "Our Father who are in Devon," he said. "Harold be Thy name." It was hysterical.'

'Any boys?' asked Lucy.

'Don't even go there. Nah. Well, one; he tried to chat me up. But he's Jeremy's younger brother so he must be a total nerd.'

'What did he look like?' asked Nesta.

'About seventeen. Quite nice-looking. Little John Lennon glasses. But wearing an awful suit that didn't fit him properly. Jeremy made him get up on the stage at the reception and play the piano. It was awful. Songs from the shows. All the oldies were singing along to *The Sound of Music, Singing in the Rain, South Pacific*. All that "Take my hand, I'm a stranger in paradise, lost in a wonderland" stuff is so naff . . .'

'My dad's got the video of *South Pacific*. My brothers do

their own version of that song,' said Lucy, then began singing: 'Take my hand, I'm a strange-looking parasite, all wrapped in a wonderloaf . . . '

'A much better version,' I said as we made our way through the market. 'So to the serious business of shopping. What do we want to look at?'

'Boys,' said Nesta.

'I'd like to get some earrings for my date with Tony,' said Lucy.

'And we must get something new for the end-of-term prom,' said Nesta. 'You never know who might be there.'

'I heard King Noz are playing,' said Lucy.

'Who are they?' I asked.

'Oh they're fantastic. They're in the Sixth Form at my brother's school. Lal's got a demo of theirs and said they may even have a recording deal.'

'Well, anything's got to be better than songs from the shows,' I said.

Camden Lock sells all sorts of paraphernalia: books, frames, joss-sticks, essential oils, crystals, jewellery, mirrors, clothes, hats, pottery, music. You name it, they sell it. The place was heaving with people browsing, buying, or meeting friends.

I wanted to do a bit of pre-Christmas shopping so I steered the girls upstairs to the New Age stalls. I thought I'd buy everyone aromatherapy oils this year.

Lucy was soon stuck in at a stall selling jewellery and Nesta was trying on sunglasses so I wandered over to a corner stall selling essential oils. I picked out the rose and jasmine bottles and had a good sniff. They're my favourite scents but also the most expensive so I haven't been able to afford them yet for my collection at home.

'Hi,' said a voice. 'Can I help?'

I glanced up and found myself staring into a pair of conker-brown eyes. Something very peculiar happened to my insides. Like someone had tied a knot in my stomach and tightened it. This boy was gorgeous. I mean *seriously* gorgeous. A wide smiley mouth and silky black hair flopping over his face.

'Er, no thanks, just looking,' I blustered, then turned and ran.

I pulled Lucy and Nesta into a corner behind a dress stall. 'I've just fallen in love,' I said breathlessly, leaning back against the wall.

'Who with?' said Nesta, sticking her head round the wall.

I pulled her back. 'Don't! He'll see.'

Lucy immediately stuck her head round the corner. 'There's a boy looking over here. Is he the one by the stairs? In a white T-shirt and jeans?'

I stuck my head out and the boy at the stall grinned and waved.

'Oh no,' I groaned, darting out of sight. 'He's seen us.

He'll think I'm a complete dork. Come on, we have to go. *Now.* Downstairs. He'll think I fancy him.'

'But you do,' said Nesta. 'What are you going to do about it?'

'Nothing,' I said and walked back into the crowds, studiously avoiding looking back at the oil stall.

When I got downstairs, Nesta and Lucy came charging after me.

'If you like him,' said Lucy, 'go and talk to him.'

'I can't. I don't know what to say. Oh God. I'm so stupid. He'll think I'm stupid.'

'No he won't,' said Nesta. 'Tell you what, we'll have a look round down here then we'll go back up and Lucy and I will go and look at the stall then kind of casually call you over to look at something.'

'Good plan,' I said. 'But you browse. I'm going to the loo to comb my hair.'

Lucy laughed. 'I told you it would happen one day, Izzie. Never say never.'

After an excruciating fifteen minutes of pretending to be interested in stalls on the ground floor, we made our way back up to the top level. I peered over the crowds and could see the boy serving someone so I went and stood with my back to him at a neighbouring stall.

Nesta and Lucy made their way over towards him.

'Lucy,' said Nesta in a mega-loud voice, 'I want to look at some aromatherapy oils.'

God. She's *so* obvious.

Lucy and Nesta were soon occupied sniffing bottles. Then Nesta said, again in her stupid loud voice, 'Izzie, come over here. Isn't one of these oils supposed to be an aphrodisiac?'

OhmyGod. Subtle is not a word in Nesta's dictionary. I turned towards them and made my way over, trying to look as cool as I could.

The boy looked up and grinned. 'Ylang ylang,' he said, offering me a bottle of oil. 'It's supposed to be a real turn-on.'

'And what do you do with it?' asked Nesta.

The boy smiled suggestively. 'Whatever you like.'

'You put a few drops in the bath,' I said sternly and sounding embarrassingly like my mother.

Nesta pulled on Lucy's arm. 'Come on, I want to look . . . er . . . over there.'

She hauled Lucy away to another stall, but not before turning back and giving me the thumbs up. Remind me to kill her later.

I looked back at the boy and grinned stupidly.

'I'm Mark,' he said, then looked in Nesta's direction and shrugged. 'Mates, huh?'

'Yeah, mates,' I said. 'I think she forgot to take her medication today. Or I forgot to take mine.'

Mark laughed. 'So you know about all this stuff, do you? Oils and that?'

'A bit. I use some of them at home, like lavender for relaxation. And eucalyptus when I've got a cold. Do you know a lot about them?'

'Not really. A bit I've picked up from my mum. I help her out here sometimes.'

'It must be great working here,' I said.

'It's OK,' shrugged Mark, then looked right into my eyes. 'You get to meet some interesting people sometimes.'

Gulp. Did he mean me? I think he did because he did that flirting thing that Nesta is always on about – holding eye contact then smiling. I felt my stomach tighten again as I looked back into his eyes.

'Look,' continued Mark, 'if you like all this stuff, there's a fair on at Alexandra Palace next week. Mind, Body and Spirit. Mum's got a stall there. Give me your number and I'll call you with the details.'

I handed him one of the cards I made in Art last term. I'm quite proud of it. I did it on turquoise paper with silver writing.

'Izzie Foster,' he said, reading the card. 'Cool. So I'll phone you later.'

Result! A date with wonderboy.

As I wandered back to the tube station with Nesta and Lucy, Christmas lights were coming on in the street and in the shops and Camden looked colourful and strangely magical. I felt like I was walking through a film set. Dusk in a perfect street in a Walt Disney world.

We linked arms and sang at the top of our voices. 'Take my hand, I'm a strange-looking parasite, all wrapped in a wonderloaf . . . thinking of yoooooou!'

# NESTA'S FLIRTING TIPS

Look into his eyes, keep contact a moment too long to show you're interested, then look away.

Smile.

Study body language: does he lean towards you, knees pointing in your direction? If he does, he's interested.

Mirror his body language.

Lean slightly towards him.

Laugh at his jokes no matter how bad they are.

Keep it fun, make small talk.

Don't get heavy.

Listen to what he's saying and look interested, fascinated even.

Don't go on about other boyfriends.

Don't be too easy.

Don't act desperate.

Don't be too available.

Don't get serious or over-emotional.

Don't be clingy.

Don't overstay your welcome. Leave when things are buzzing. That way, he'll want to come back to you for more.

<u>To check if he's interested</u>: Make eye contact that moment too long as in tip 1, then hide behind a pillar where you can see him. Watch to see if he looks to where you were last standing and, seeing you gone, looks round for you. If he does, he's interested.

# Chapter 3

# Boy
## Speak

'When a boy says he'll phone you later, what does that mean?' I asked Nesta and Lucy as we made our way to class the following Wednesday.

'Ah,' said Nesta, 'tricky one.'

'It means later, *much* later, not like a girl,' said Lucy. 'When a girl says I'll phone you later, she means later, like that night. But boys have a language all of their own.'

'I take it Mark hasn't phoned yet?' said Nesta.

I shook my head.

'Early days,' said Lucy, looking at me sympathetically. 'He'll phone. He said he would.'

Nesta shook her head. 'That means nothing in boy speak. "I'll phone you" could mean anything. I'll phone you in a week, in two weeks, next month. If I remember.'

I groaned. 'Oh no. It's agony and it's only been three

days. I stayed up late every night hoping he'd call but zilch.'

'He'd never phone that soon,' said Nesta, 'not if he's cool. It would make him look too keen. Give it a day or so and even then don't hold your breath.'

I do love Nesta but sometimes I wish she wouldn't say exactly what she means all the time.

'A watched phone never rings,' said Lucy sagely.

'Tell me about it,' I said as I took my place at my desk. 'But he has to phone in the next couple of days as the fair at Ally Pally is on Saturday.'

School has been a riot this week and a welcome distraction from waiting for the phone call. We have a student teacher called Miss Hartley standing in for our regular PHSE and RE teacher Miss Watkins. As usual, poor thing, she's live bait for some of our class who like nothing better than to give trainee teachers a hard time.

First class she took was Religious Education. I usually enjoy RE as we've been doing all the different belief systems from all over the world. I find it fascinating finding out what different cultures think. Last term I was a Hindu. They believe that you have many lives, not just one, that our souls change bodies when we die and we come back as someone else.

I made a badge saying *Reincarnation's making a come-back*, which I wore to school until Mrs Allen saw it and told me to take it off. It was nice though, thinking I might have known people in another life. One day I asked Nesta if she thought we had known each other before.

'Oh definitely,' she said.

'What, as your sister or something?' I asked.

'No,' she said, 'you were my pet frog.'

Then Lucy piped up in her daft Scottish accent, 'What does a Hindu?' She waited for our answer. 'Lays eggs,' she giggled. 'Geddit? *Hen*-du?'

Nesta and Lucy think it's all one big joke and don't seem to realise that I really want to know about stuff like why we're here and what it's all about. Though I have decided to stop being a Hindu and be an agnostic until I decide for definite.

Miss Hartley coughed to get our attention then began. 'OK, class, today we're going to talk about God. What do we know about him?'

'Omnipresent, omnipotent, omniscient,' said Jade Wilcocks.

'Very good,' said Miss Hartley.

'Best-selling author,' said Mary O'Connor. 'He wrote the Bible.'

The class started sniggering so I put my hand up.

'Izzie?'

'Well actually, miss, I have a question about God.'

I'd been thinking about it ever since the wedding on Saturday when the priest had said, 'Here we are gathered in the presence of God . . .'

'If God is omnipresent, that means God is everywhere, doesn't it?'

'Yes,' said Miss Hartley.

'Then why do people go to church to pray? If he's omnipresent, wouldn't we be in his presence everywhere? In the cinema, at home? Everywhere? Why go to a church?'

'Good point, Izzie,' said Miss Hartley. 'Anyone else like to comment?'

'Miss, if he's everywhere, does that mean he's watching you when you go to the toilet?' asked Candice Carter.

Oh no. They were off. Wind-up time and I was hoping to get some answers to my questions.

'Why do people pray to the ceiling if he's everywhere?' said Joanne Richards. 'You could just as well pray under the sink.'

Quite right, I thought. I put my hand up again.

'Miss, if he's omnipresent and people are always praying to him, how does he hear everyone at the same time? Does he have an exchange system? It must be hard with all the millions of prayers coming in in all the different languages. He may speak only Swahili for all we know.'

Miss Hartley was beginning to look a bit flustered.

'Anyone else got anything to say?'

I put my hand up again. I had loads to say as I think a lot about things like this.

'Do you think maybe God is in a bit of a bad mood

because being omnipresent isn't as much fun as it used to be when the world was new and fresh? Like, being everywhere all the time, he has to watch *all* the repeats of *Neighbours* every day, plus all the repeats, in all the languages, in all the different countries, for eternity. It must get very boring.'

'Is eternity like a Sunday when it's raining?' asked Lucy.

'Good questions,' said Miss Hartley, avoiding the answers. 'Maybe you could write an essay for next week on how you see God. Now get out your Bibles.'

I was still wondering how God answered prayers. But maybe he's like Mark. Doesn't call back. Now that got me thinking again.

I stuck my hand up again. 'Miss, why do we call God a he? Why not a she? Or an it?'

'I think we'll call you Izzie Why Foster from now on,' said Miss Hartley. 'Why why why?'

She obviously doesn't know as she didn't bother to try to answer. 'Now, class, who can name some of the famous characters in the hymns we sing in assembly?'

'Gabriel,' said Mary.

'Lucifer,' said Jade.

'Er, no,' said Miss Hartley, 'that's another name for the devil. He was a fallen angel.'

'Fallen from where?' I asked before she could tell me to shut up.

'Heaven,' she said.

'Devon,' whispered Lucy behind me. 'And Harold is his name.'

I got the giggles then and decided to give up on my next question which was, 'And where exactly is heaven?'

'I've got a character out of a hymn,' said Candice Carter.

'OK,' said Miss Hartley.

'Hark, miss.'

'And in which hymn is there a reference to a character called Hark, Candice?'

'Hark, the Herald Angel, miss.'

There was no stopping the class after that. Even Nesta joined in.

'I've got one, miss.'

'OK, Nesta, go ahead.'

'Gladly, miss.'

By now poor Miss Hartley was looking as though she wished she could be anywhere else but that classroom.

'Gladly,' she said wearily. 'Who was he?'

'Gladly the cross-eyed bear, miss.'

The whole class fell about laughing as we all know Gladly well, but being new to the school, Miss Hartley didn't get the joke.

Candice put her hand up. 'It's one of the ancient hymns we sing in assembly, miss. It starts, "Gladly the cross I bear".'

Miss Hartley still didn't laugh. The bell for break went

a moment later and she was out of the class and down the corridor before any of us.

At lunch-time, I checked my mobile. No messages, so I called home and punched in the code numbers to check the answering machine. Nothing. Then an *awful* thought struck me. Mum got me a new mobile a month ago and I made the cards *two* months ago. *Oh no.* The mobile number on the card I gave Mark was the old one.

'He won't call in the day,' said Lucy. 'He'll be at school.'

'You're right,' I sighed. 'But he'll probably call tonight.'

'But tonight you're coming back to our house with Nesta, aren't you? Mum and Dad are going to a movie and we're going to watch a video.'

'Sorry, Lucy, I don't want to miss the call.'

Lucy looked disappointed. 'You haven't been back one night this week. Oh, come on, Izzie, the machine will keep any messages.'

I thought Lucy of all people would understand, being so in love with Tony. But she didn't.

# BOY SPEAK

| | |
|---|---|
| Call you later: | Sometime in the next century |
| Commitment: | A word only applied to a football team |
| I need space: | For all my other girlfriends |
| Let's just see how it goes: | Back off, I'm feeling pressured |
| Would you like a back rub?: | I want to try my luck |
| Isn't it warm in here?: | Take your clothes off |
| Hi. Your friend looks nice: | I fancy her and am using you to get to her |
| Don't get heavy: | I don't feel the same way about you |
| She's ugly/a lesbian: | She didn't fancy me |
| I'm not ready for a relationship: | Not with you, anyway |
| I'm very independent: | I like to do things my own way, on my own terms |
| We can still be friends: | It's over and this is probably the last time you'll ever see me |

# Chapter 4

# Consulting
# the Stars

Wednesday night: no call.

Thursday lunch-time: no call.

Thursday night: no call.

Friday morning: no call.

I'm going out of my mind. Perhaps he lost my number? Perhaps he put the card in his jeans and his mum washed them and it got soaked? Perhaps he didn't mean to call at all and saying he would was a way of getting rid of me? Perhaps, perhaps, perhaps.

It's time to consult the oracles.

I sent Lucy a note in English.

*Will you come back to my house tonight? I want to look at my horoscope and do the tarot cards to see what they have to say about Mark. I know Nesta's busy with Drama but can you come?*

*Sure,* Lucy wrote back. *But it's my turn to feed the dogs. We can do it on the way. I won't be long.*

'Izzie Foster, Lucy Lovering, pay attention,' said Mr Johnson, 'and get out your folders. Today I want you to write something about school. How you feel about it. It can be in any form you like: an essay, a poem, whatever. You've got twenty minutes. And no talking.'

I spent the first ten minutes gazing out of the window, hoping for inspiration, but all I could think about was Mark. I was trying to picture what he looked like, as already his face had gone blurry in my mind. Maybe he wasn't as good-looking as I remembered. Maybe I'd see him again and it would be like, Yuk, what did I ever see in you? I wondered what he's really like. What kind of music he's into.

'Izzie Foster, have you written anything yet?' asked Mr Johnson.

'Er, no, sir.'

I looked at the blank sheet in front of me and put my mind to the exercise in hand. An essay about school. How boring. Then I remembered, he'd said it could be any form at all. I want to be a songwriter when I leave school – well, either that or an astrologer, and maybe both. I've written loads of songs at home so I decided

I'd do one here. I put my head down and started writing.

After another ten minutes, Mr Johnson clapped his hands.

'OK, time's up. And seeing as it took you so long to get going, Izzie, let's hear what you've come up with.'

Oh NO. *NO*. I never show anyone my lyrics. Ever. They're completely private. He never said we had to read them out loud.

'We're waiting,' said Mr Johnson, tapping his fingers on his desk.

I stood up. 'It's a rap song. Called "Education Rap",' I said, then began reading:

*'Now I'm walkin' down the street with my feet on the beat, An' I look real cool cos I ain't no fool, I go to school . . . '*

Immediately Mary O'Connor and Joanne Richards started sniggering. I felt myself freeze and stopped reading immediately.

'Er, that's all I've written, sir,' I muttered to the floor. It wasn't. I'd written a whole verse but I didn't want to read more if people were going to laugh at me.

I looked up at Mr Johnson. He seemed to be laughing as well. 'Hmmm, an interesting start,' he said.

I sat down feeling miserable. Never again. Never ever ever again. No one's ever going to see my lyrics, not if they're going to make fun.

* * *

'I thought your song was great,' said Lucy as we let ourselves in the back door at her house.

'Thanks,' I said as one of the dogs pounced forward to lick my face, almost knocking me over. 'Down, Ben, down.'

'I won't be long,' said Lucy as she took off her coat and started rummaging in a cupboard for tins of dog food. 'Put the kettle on.'

'But we're not staying long, are we? Got to get home, remember?'

'Oh right,' said Lucy. 'Mark.'

'Yeah. Mark,' I said. I was getting seriously concerned by now. It was Friday night and the fair was Saturday and Mark still hadn't phoned. 'Who's playing the guitar?'

Music was coming from the living-room so I followed the direction of the sounds and found Lucy's brother Lal lying on the sofa listening to a CD.

'Who's this?' I asked.

'King Noz,' said Lal.

'Oh yeah, Lucy mentioned them, they're playing at our end-of-term prom.'

'Yeah,' said Lal. 'They go to our school. Top band.'

'Can I listen?'

'Sure.'

A boy was singing with an acoustic guitar and piano accompaniment. I sat back on the sofa, closed my eyes and listened to the lyrics.

*'If you were a wheel*
*I'd follow your highway.*
*If you were a raindrop*
*I wish you'd fall my way.*
*If you were a gypsy*
*I'd give a fortune to tell*
*That whenever I'm with you*
*I see heaven, not hell . . . '*

'Wow,' I said when he'd finished. 'He's really good. I really like it.'

'Not all of it is quiet like that,' said Lal. 'I prefer the heavier numbers.'

'Ready,' called Lucy.

'Got to go,' I said, getting up. The stars were calling.

When we got back home, I checked the machine for messages. Nothing. *Nothing.*

'Never mind,' said Lucy. 'I have a surprise for you.'

We went up to my bedroom and she handed me an envelope.

'What is it?' I asked.

'Look and see.'

I ripped open the envelope and there were three tickets to the Mind, Body and Spirit fair the next day.

'Fabola!' I said. 'Where did you get these?'

'Dad,' said Lucy. 'He has a stall there selling his health foods. He gave them to us so we can all get in for free. So even if Mark doesn't phone tonight, we can go anyway, check out where his mum's stall is, then accidentally-on-purpose bump into him.'

I gave Lucy a huge hug. So she *did* understand how much it meant to me after all. 'Excellent. Lucy, you really are a pal.'

Lucy beamed. 'Well, come on, let's see what our horoscopes are. I'm dying to know, as I'm seeing Tony tomorrow night and want to know if it's going to go well.'

I switched on my computer and went to my favourite website. I typed in my and Lucy's birth dates and waited for the horoscopes to print out.

'Where are you going with him?' I asked.

'Hollywood Bowl,' Lucy replied. 'We're going to see a movie then going to get a burger or something after.'

'You really like him, don't you?' I asked.

Lucy grinned. 'Oh yeah, oh *yeah.*'

'But you'll be careful, won't you? Nesta's not the only one worried that he might hurt you.'

'Gimme a break,' said Lucy. 'I know what he's like. Nesta's told me enough times.'

I picked up the sheets of paper from the printer and began to read.

'What does it say?' asked Lucy.

'This is amazing,' I said. 'This explains *everything*. It says that Mercury has been retrograde but moves direct on the sixth of December. That's tomorrow.'

'What does that mean?' asked Lucy.

'Well Mercury's the planet of communication. Whenever it turns retrograde, it slows down all kinds of things. Misunderstandings happen, appointments get double-booked, you can't get through to people you need to talk to, all that kind of stuff. Then when it turns direct, it all starts flowing again. So don't you see? That's why Mark didn't phone. Because Mercury was retrograde.'

'Do you really think the stars influence us that much?' asked Lucy doubtfully.

'Oh absolutely,' I said, reading on. 'Oh this is fantastic, for both of us. Venus is well aspected tomorrow with a full Moon in Taurus. . .'

'Izzie,' said Lucy, 'you're talking gobbledygook to me. Explain.'

'Venus is the planet of love. It rules the star sign of Taurus. It couldn't be better placed tomorrow. It looks like we're both in for a good time. Top. I can't wait. I'm going to mark all the dates on my diary when the stars are well aspected. I don't know why I've put myself through such hell this week. I should have consulted the site in the beginning then I wouldn't have been through such misery.'

Lucy was still looking doubtful. 'I'm sure there's more to it than that,' she said.

'Nonsense,' I said, feeling better than I had for days. 'Astrology rules, OK?'

'Oh,' laughed Lucy. 'OK.'

At that moment, the bedroom door opened.

'Supper's on the table,' said Mum. 'Would you like some, Lucy?'

'Oh, yes please,' said Lucy. 'I'd love some.'

'Can we have ours up here?' I asked. 'Please, Mum?'

'OK,' said Mum. 'Seeing as Lucy's here. I'll bring a tray up. But be sure to eat at the desk and not off your laps.'

When she'd gone, I got up and shut the door. 'Honestly, it drives me mad. She won't let me have a lock on my door. She doesn't even knock. I have no privacy. She's always bursting in when I'm doing things. Nesta's allowed a lock on her door. Why shouldn't I be?'

'I know,' Lucy said. 'I've asked for a lock on my door too but Mum and Dad said no way. What if something happened to me? Durrh, like what exactly? Sometimes parents have overactive imaginations.'

Mum came back a few minutes later carrying a tray with two plates of shepherd's pie. 'There you are, Izzie, your favourite.'

I pulled a face. 'Mum, you know I don't eat meat any more.'

Mum put the tray down. 'Oh for heaven's sake, Isobel. I can't keep up.' She turned on Lucy. 'And have you stopped eating meat as well, Lucy?'

'Er, no,' said Lucy, taking the plate. 'I love shepherd's pie, thank you very much, Mrs Foster.'

Mum turned to leave. 'Well, see if you can talk some sense into Little Miss Contrary here. Because, Izzie, I've had enough. I made it specially. So if you don't eat that, you don't eat anything.'

Lucy pulled a silly face when she'd gone. 'Little Miss Contrary. Don't worry, I'll eat yours.'

'I'll eat the potato and vegetables. And you can have the meat. I don't know why she won't give me a break. Honestly. It's not like I'm being difficult or anything. I just believe you are what you eat.'

'Mooo,' giggled Lucy through a mouthful of minced beef.

'God you're daft at times,' I said, but I couldn't help laughing. 'Now let's plan what we're going to wear for the fair.'

# EDUCATION RAP

Now I'm walking down the street with my feet on the
   beat,
An' I look real cool cos I ain't no fool, I go to school.
Don't wanna be a loser, a street corner boozer, a bum
   for rum or a no-hope dope.
Now I'm really going places, I'm holdin' all aces,
I got smart cos I know in my heart I got a real good
   start,
I'm ahead of the pack, no lookin' back, I'm goin' up
   don't need no luck,
Cos I ain't no fool, I go to school.

# Chapter 5

# Ready for Action

I woke up feeling like it was Christmas day already. I felt so excited – today was the big day. But first I needed breakfast. I was ravenous after not having had much dinner the night before. Sometimes it's hard being healthy, as there's one thing I do like and that's my food. I'd been dreaming of it all night – deep pan pizza with pepperoni topping, roast chicken, and stodgy treacle pudding. Lovely.

I went down to the kitchen and searched the cupboards to see what I could find that was nutritious. Before I knew it, I'd woolfed down three slices of white toast with mashed banana. At least the banana bit was healthy. I'd have to buy some wholemeal bread at the fair. They'd be bound to have stalls selling it. And maybe Mum'd get the message if I brought some back and left it for her in the bread-bin. In the meantime, I'd have to compromise. Another piece of toast.

With maybe a dollop of that lovely chocolate spread on it.

After breakfast, I took a long bath with my special bubble bath for relaxation, then went to change into the clothes that Lucy and I had picked out last night – my black top and mini skirt, red tights and a red headband. With bright scarlet lips as the final touch, I thought the whole effect looked pretty cool.

I hope my bum doesn't look too big in this skirt, I thought as I put on my ankle boots. I took a last check in the mirror and thankfully the boots made my legs look a bit longer so I guessed I'd have to do.

I grabbed my leather jacket and was ready. Get ready, Mark, because here I come!

'I'm off to Ally Pally,' I called to Mum as I came down the stairs.

'OK, love, have a good time,' she said, coming out into the hall. 'Have you got enough money?'

'Yes, thanks. I've got my Christmas savings.'

And then she saw me and her face dropped.

'Where do you think you're going dressed like that?'

'I told you. Ally Pally.' I prayed she wasn't going to make a fuss. I was meeting Lucy and Nesta in Muswell Hill at ten thirty.

'Back up those stairs this instant.'

'But *why*?'

'You're not going anywhere in that skirt. You're showing everything you've got.'

'But Mum . . . '

'*Now,* Izzie. And wipe that lipstick off. It's far too bright for someone your age. And put some warmer tights on, those are too thin for this weather.'

I sighed and turned back upstairs. I took off the tights and mini-skirt and put on my usual long black skirt. She couldn't object to that, it comes right down to the floor. But before leaving, I stuffed the mini skirt and red tights into a carrier bag and shoved them in my bag.

'OK now?' I said to Mum as I went back downstairs.

'Much better,' Mum smiled. 'Have a nice time.'

When we got up to Alexandra Palace we stood and admired the view for a moment. It was a rare clear day and you could see for miles over London, right out to Docklands.

'This place is really cool,' said Nesta as we walked up the steps and into the vast reception hall. It was a huge conservatory with a glass ceiling and the most enormous palm plants I'd ever seen. In the middle of the hall there was a choir singing Christmas carols.

Lucy and Nesta listened to the choir while I went into the ladies', put my mini skirt and tights on and reapplied my lipstick.

'Wow,' said Nesta when I went out to join her and Lucy. 'You look hot.'

I grinned. 'Ready for action.'

'Ready for action!' echoed the girls.

The main hall was heaving with people. First stop was Mr L's stall to thank him for the tickets. Mr L is our nickname for Lucy's dad; he doesn't seem to mind.

'Hi, Izzie,' he said. 'You're looking . . . striking.'

'Thanks, Mr L. And thanks for the tickets.'

'Pleasure,' he said. 'And how's the guitar playing coming along?'

'Good,' I said. 'I've been practising hard.'

Lucy's dad looks like an old hippie with his ponytail. He used to be in a band back in the Seventies and still plays a bit at some jazz club in Crouch End but he also gives people lessons. I go every other week and he's really helped me improve.

'Lucy tells me that you've opted to follow a more healthy diet,' he said.

'Yeah.'

'Well I hope you're doing it properly, Izzie. A lot of people change their diet but don't eat the right sorts of foods. You need plenty of grains, lentils, that sort of thing . . . '

Yurgh, I thought, no way I'm eating lentils. But I wasn't really listening as Mr L carried on about nutrients and soya products. I wanted to get going, cruising the hall and looking for Mark.

'Do you know where the stalls selling essential oils are?' I asked.

'Over by the back wall,' said Mr L. 'I think they've put

all that sort of thing together so people can find them easily.'

'Brill, thanks,' I said. 'See you later.'

We made our way over to the area he'd said and I made sure that Lucy, Nesta and I were laughing so that if Mark saw me, he'd see what a good time I was having and realise what a fun person I am.

'What did Good King Wenceslas say when he phoned the Pizza Hut and they asked what he wanted?' I asked.

'What?' said Lucy.

'The usual – deep pan, crisp and even,' I replied, throwing my head back in what I thought was an attractive manner and laughing.

Nesta and Lucy looked at me a bit oddly.

'You OK, Izzie?' asked Lucy.

'Oh yes,' I said, laughing hysterically. 'It's just *sooo* funny.'

Lucy and Nesta exchanged worried looks.

'She's cracking up,' said Nesta.

'Literally,' said Lucy.

When we got to the aromatherapy area, I suddenly got the most awful attack of butterflies.

'What if he didn't phone on purpose? Didn't want to see me?'

'Oh come on,' said Nesta, dragging me into the aisle. 'There's only one way to find out.'

We started looking at the first stall. The man behind it was bald and in his fifties. The second stall was run by a couple of middle-aged ladies. Third stall, another man. Fourth stall, two young girls.

'Can you remember what brand of oils Mark's mum sold?' asked Lucy. 'Any of these could be his stall and he hasn't arrived yet.'

'No,' I groaned as I looked up the aisle. 'And any one of these people could be his mum or his dad.'

By the time we got to the end of the aisle, we'd seen about twelve stalls, some selling oils, some bath lotions, some burners, some books. But there was no sign of Mark.

'We're going to have to do the whole hall,' sighed Nesta. 'Maybe his mum's stall has been put somewhere else.'

I looked around. The hall was enormous; there had to be about three hundred, if not more, different stalls.

'It's going to take ages,' I said. 'Look, why don't we split up? We've all got our mobiles. If you see him, call. If not, meet at the big clock at about one o'clock.'

'OK,' said Lucy. 'Let's synchronise watches.'

We all checked our watches.

'Right, let's go,' said Nesta.

This wasn't part of my plan. Now the chances were he'd spot me on my own like some desperate saddo, wandering about looking for him. I began to think perhaps I shouldn't have gone at all.

As I searched my area, I couldn't help but be drawn into

what was on sale. Really good stuff. I bought some organic bread and muesli, then a rose quartz pendulum for my mum. I decided I'd wear it just for the afternoon as the lady selling them told me that the stones soothe the nervous system and dispel fear. Just what I need at the moment, I thought, as each time I turned a corner the butterflies came back. I also bought a book on Feng Shui and thought I could do my bedroom when I got home.

I was just talking to a man about some detox potion when my phone rang. My heart lurched. Lucy or Nesta must have spotted Mark.

'I'm going to the clock,' said Nesta. 'I've looked everywhere and there's no sign of the culprit.'

My heart sank. I looked at my watch. An hour had gone by already.

'No show,' said Lucy when I got to the clock. 'Why don't we go and get a hot chocolate?'

We wandered to the snack bar where I bought the girls chocolates to thank them for their efforts and got myself a herb tea.

'Ergh,' said Nesta, smelling the cup. 'How can you drink that stuff? It smells like washing-up water.'

I took a sip and had to agree but I was determined to stay with my new regime no matter what.

'I don't think he's coming,' I said. 'So much for Venus being well aspected today.'

'It's not over yet,' said Lucy. 'Don't give up on him just yet.'

'No,' said Nesta. '*Do* give up. I reckon it's when you give up that things happen.'

'Thanks a lot! Give up, don't give up . . . ' I laughed. 'Rotten pair of agony aunts you two would make.'

'Let's just enjoy being here for a while,' said Nesta. 'Forget all about Mark for now.'

'Don't have much choice, do I?' I said.

We spent the next couple of hours having a good wander and trying out all the different things on offer. Nesta had an Indian head massage and Lucy and I had a reflexology session which was really nice but Lucy ended up giggling as she said it tickled. Best was a massage chair which you sat in and it massaged up and down your back with rollers. It was wonderful and any other day I would have loved being at the fair, but I couldn't help feeling disappointed. Mark hadn't phoned and he hadn't come. The first time I see a boy I like and I don't even get the chance to get to know him and dazzle him with my brilliant personality.

'Maybe something's happened to him,' I said. 'Perhaps he's had an accident.'

'Perhaps he's just a boy,' said Nesta. 'Unreliable. Forget him.'

'And I have to go soon,' said Lucy. 'I have to get ready for tonight.'

'Me too,' grinned Nesta.

'Why? Where are you going?' I asked.

'Baby-sitting.'

'You baby-sitting? Why?' I asked. I knew Nesta didn't need to earn extra pocket money as her parents gave her a very generous allowance. There had to be an ulterior motive.

'Yeah, me baby-sitting,' she said. 'For our next-door neighbour.'

'And?' I asked.

'And,' said Nesta, 'it just happens that their oldest son Nathan will be back for the weekend from university.'

'Why can't he baby-sit?' asked Lucy.

'He's going to some concert in town,' explained Nesta. 'That's why I said I'd do it. I want to see him before he goes.'

'Why? Do you fancy him?' asked Lucy.

'Nah,' said Nesta. 'But he does go to university in Scotland. And a young man I have my eye on will be studying there. I'm hoping Nathan'll get to know him and introduce me.'

'This is the first you've told us,' I said. 'What young man?'

'You may have seen him at the Oscars . . .' said Nesta.

'No way!'

'Yeah,' said Nesta. 'Why not? You have to aim high.'

'Yeah, you and every A-list celeb,' I said. 'Wasn't Blake Lively texting him at one time?'

Nesta nodded. 'Yeah, but I think I'm much more his type.'

Despite my disappointment at not seeing Mark, I had

to laugh. If there's one thing Nesta's not short of, that's confidence.

After the girls had gone, I mooched around for a while by myself, looking for Christmas presents for Lucy and Nesta. With still an hour to kill before the end of the fair, I had a henna tattoo done on my ankle. A delicate bracelet of leaves, it looked really cool.

'I hope my mum doesn't freak out too much,' I said to the woman painting it on.

'Oh don't worry. They only last a few weeks, then if you want it done again, you can come to our shop in Kentish Town and have it redone. Or pick another design.'

'Fab,' I said, then had an idea. I could buy Nesta and Lucy one for Christmas. They'd love them.

'I don't understand why people have permanent ones done,' continued the woman, 'when they can get one of these instead. They look just as good. And tastes change. If it's permanent, you can't do much about it except laser it off, which can be painful and expensive.'

After my tattoo, I bought a toe-ring and some organic chocolate, then some love charms from a rather strange woman on another stall. By now, most of the stallholders were packing up and the crowds were beginning to disperse.

He's not coming, I thought. I might as well go.

Feeling let down and dejected, I changed back into my

long skirt and made my way out of the hall and down the hill to the bus stop.

Get a grip, I told myself as I sat on the bus. It's not like you even know Mark. In fact, to tell the truth, I couldn't even remember what he looked like very clearly. I'd got myself in a state about nothing. I decided to think about a new song. Making up lyrics always makes me feel better and I decided I'd think about a subject far removed from boys and love and heartache. At the beginning of term, we had a class about all the countries in the world that didn't have enough to eat. I told Lucy I was going to write a song for Africa and as I sat on the bus thinking about it, words started buzzing round my head.

By the time the bus reached my stop, I was feeling more like my old self. I'd finish my song when I got home, I decided, then watch a soppy DVD with my bar of organic chocolate. Perfecto. Boys! Phfff! Who needs 'em?

As I walked past the shops towards our road, I noticed a bunch of lads walking towards me. They were all dressed in muddy football gear and I decided I'd cross the road to avoid them. I knew what boys could be like in a group when they see a girl on her own and I wasn't in the mood for any comments, even nice ones. Then my heart stopped. One of the boys was Mark.

What should I do? Oh God. They were getting closer. I couldn't resist. I'd stay on that side of the road and see what he did.

The gang of lads walked past all engrossed in some conversation about the game they'd just played. I looked straight at Mark, waiting to see how he'd respond.

I couldn't believe it. He *blanked* me.

I carried on walking, feeling numb. He'd blanked me. Oh God. I couldn't wait to get home to my bedroom where I could hide.

As I turned the corner into our road, I heard footsteps running behind me.

I hurried my own pace. It was dark, and by now I was desperate to get home. I leaped as a hand grabbed my shoulder.

I swung round, ready to kick as hard as I could.

It was Mark.

'Hey,' he said. 'Don't I know you from somewhere?'

From *somewhere*? I thought. He doesn't even know who I am, the creep.

'The Lock, last Saturday,' I said.

'Sorry about back then on the road,' he said. 'I didn't want to let on I knew you as all my mates would start asking questions and, well, you know how it can be . . . '

I didn't, but I was beginning to soften. He was even better-looking than I remembered, even though he was splattered in mud and his hair was all over the place. Gorgeous eyes with silky long lashes.

He grinned sheepishly. 'I was supposed to phone you, wasn't I? About the fair.'

'Were you?' I said. 'I don't remember.'

'Yeah. You gave me your card. Pretty turquoise one with silver writing.'

So he did remember.

He dived in his sports bag and pulled out a wallet.

'See? I've got it here.'

'Got a pen?' I said, trying to stay as cool as possible.

'No.'

'No matter, I've got one,' I said, quickly rooting round in my bag. I took my card back from him and scribbled my new number on it. 'One of the numbers has changed. I got a new mobile since I made those cards.'

'Oh, right,' he said, taking the card and putting it back in his wallet. 'Anyway, did you go? To Ally Pally?'

'No,' I lied. I wasn't about to let on I'd spent the day looking for him. 'Did you go?' I asked.

'Nah,' he said. 'My sister said she'd do the stall with Mum for me. She loves all that kind of thing.' He shifted awkwardly then smiled widely. 'Look. Sorry I didn't call. This week's been mad. How about I give you a call next week and we go out sometime?'

My heart leaped. He *was* interested. I shrugged, not wanting to appear too easy. 'Yeah, maybe,' I said.

At that moment, his mates appeared at the end of the road, 'Oi, Mark, you coming or what?' one of them yelled.

'Look, Izzie Foster, got to go. I'll call you. Promise.' And with that he ran off.

I felt stunned. He even remembered my name. So my horoscope was right after all. Venus was well aspected, even if it took its time to get going. And Nesta was right too. When you give up, things do start happening.

# SONG FOR AFRICA
## by Izzie Foster

Cracked lips, parched land,
Dusty promises of help at hand.
Hungry children on Christmas cards
Won't help a world that's growing too fast.

I just wish it would rain on Africa.

But storm clouds gathering won't bring relief,
Just darker days with no hope of peace in Africa.

I just wish it would rain on Africa.
Wash out the pain of Africa.

Guns and bombs, tears and mud,
Luxury limos race through blood.
But bound by debt to hopelessness
Can we ever clean this mess?

I just wish it would rain on Africa.
Wash out the pain of Africa.

# Chapter 6

# Love
# Spells

Cool. I am the Queen of it. I consulted my horoscope and, it said the week would get off to a slow start but things would start moving again on Friday. And Venus was in a good place for a romantic weekend. Top. Sounded like Mark would phone at the end of the week and I'd see him on Saturday or Sunday.

The week at school flew by and it was such a relief not to be in a flap about waiting for the phone. He'd promised he'd ring, and as Nesta said, you have to give them time.

However, by Friday the same old feelings were beginning to creep back.

'So what exactly did he say?' asked Lucy.

'That he'd call next week.'

'Well that could be any day till Sunday,' said Nesta. 'Chill.'

It was all right for her, she didn't fancy anyone special. And whenever she did have her eye on someone, they always seemed to call. Lucy, on the other hand, was anything but chilled. Her date with Tony had gone really well and she was seeing him again that evening after school. She was so excited.

'Though he still keeps saying I might be a bit young for him,' she said.

'Probably because he wants to grope you,' said Nesta. 'And knows I'll kill him if he does.'

'No,' insisted Lucy. 'He's not like that, honest.'

Nesta looked at me and raised an eyebrow. She clearly had her doubts and I have to say, I shared her concern.

I dashed home on Friday night and waited for the call. I kept busy watching *EastEnders* then a DVD but by nine thirty, I was beginning to think Mark wasn't going to call.

I rang Lucy and asked her to phone both our home phone and my mobile to check that both were working.

The downstairs phone rang a minute later.

'Home phone working,' said Lucy. 'I'll try the mobile now.'

A moment later my mobile rang. 'Lucy again,' she said. 'It looks like it's all in order. And Izzie, have you got a minute? I need to talk to you.'

It suddenly occurred to me that Mark might be trying to get through at just that moment so I didn't want to have a long conversation.

'Can it wait?' I asked. 'Mark might be trying to get through.'

'OK,' she said, sounding disappointed. 'I'll talk to you tomorrow but not when Nesta's around. OK?'

After she put the phone down I felt a bit rotten as I remembered she was supposed to have seen Tony after school. She probably wanted to talk about that and didn't feel she could open up with Nesta there seeing as he's her brother. I hoped she was OK and made a mental note to make it up to her tomorrow.

There was nothing else on TV I wanted to watch so I got out my love charms from the fair and decided to try one out to see if that would help the phone to ring.

'Charm to make a boy sweet on you,' I read. 'Write your love's name on a piece of paper, then sprinkle it with sugar and put it under your pillow and sleep on it.'

I found a piece of purple writing paper and thought that would be the best to use, as purple is a magical colour. I wrote Mark's name on it in a heart then went down to the kitchen and rooted in the cupboards for sugar.

Brown or white? I wondered. Does it matter? I settled for the brown and sprinkled it liberally on my paper. Luckily Mum and Angus were next door watching TV, as they would think I was barking if they'd caught me.

I took my charm back upstairs and put it under my pillow. Immediately the phone rang. Amazing. It worked! I dashed down to the hall to answer it.

'Is Dad there?' said Claudia's voice.

'Yes,' I said. 'I'll get him. But don't be long, I'm expecting an important phone call.'

I hovered on the upstairs landing as Angus took his call. *Ten minutes!* Mark could have been trying to get through and Claudia would have ruined everything. What we clearly needed in our house was Call Waiting, so that you could tell if someone was trying to get through when you were on the line. I must put it on my Christmas list, I thought, along with a lock for my bedroom door.

After they'd finished talking I went back into my bedroom to read but I couldn't really concentrate as my mind spiralled into maybes again. Maybe this time he really had lost my number. Maybe, maybe, maybe, zzzzz.

I must have dozed off at some point because the next thing I knew, it was Saturday morning and my mobile was ringing.

Oh thank God, I thought as I picked it up.

'Izzie, it's me,' said Nesta. 'Has Mark called yet?'

'No,' I replied. 'Do you think I should go to the Lock to see if he's working there today?'

'NO!' wailed Nesta. 'No, no, *no*. Anyway, Lucy and I had a long talk about you this morning. We're both worried. What would you say if he's at the Lock?'

'Well I could say I was Christmas shopping again.'

'No, Izzie. I won't let you. It'll be really obvious. You'd look desperate and if there's one things boys hate, it's desperate.

Honest, Izzie, you're losing the plot. What's come over you? It's usually you telling Lucy this stuff.'

'I know. I hope she's going to be OK with your brother.'

'*Don't* try and change the subject,' said Nesta. 'We're talking about you and how you're not going to the Lock today.'

'Oh come on, Nesta, come with me. I'd do it for you.'

'No. You'd be all weird if you did see him, wondering if he was going to call or not. You won't be yourself. He'll pick up on it. And what if he wasn't there like the fair last week? You'll only feel down.'

'So what should we do, then?' I asked. I knew better than to argue with Miss Know-It-All when she's in a mood like this.

'Lucy and I are going to meet in Hampstead. See you there in half an hour.'

'OK,' I said. 'But I can't stay long, I have to go to my dad's later.'

Nesta and Lucy did their best to cheer me up, but I was sure that I'd blown it with Mark. I'd gone over everything I'd said to him a million times.

'I just know he's not going to phone. I think I was a bit off with him when I saw him last Saturday. He probably thinks I'm not interested.'

'Relax, Izzie,' said Nesta. 'You're over-analysing.'

We were sitting in a café on Hampstead High Street and

Nesta and Lucy were drinking cappuccinos while I sipped on a camomile tea.

'My life is over,' I said. 'I will never have a boyfriend. I will be alone all my life. And I've got a big bum.'

Lucy started laughing. We always played a game when one of us was having a moan. Who could outdo the others with the worst life. 'Ah,' she said, 'but I look twelve when I'm fourteen.'

'Not since you had your hair cut,' said Nesta. 'You look at least twelve and a half now . . . '

Lucy pinched her. 'Excuse me! I haven't finished my tale of woe. My parents are mad hippies.'

'I think your parents are cool,' I said. 'I wish they were mine. That's another thing to add to my list. I have the most boring mother and stepfather in the world.'

'OK, my turn,' said Nesta. 'I'm five foot seven and all the local boys are midgets.'

'Well, what does that matter if you're going to marry a movie star? They're usually tall!'

When Nesta went downstairs to go to the loo, Lucy suddenly looked really serious.

'Izzie, I have to talk to you,' she said. 'About Tony.'

'What?'

She shifted uncomfortably. 'Well, you know what I was saying about him thinking I was too young for him? Well Nesta was right.'

'What, about him wanting to grope you?'

Lucy nodded. 'I don't know what to do. I mean, up till now we've just snogged but last night he said he wants to take it further.'

'Oh God,' I said. 'What are you going to do?'

'Dunno. I don't want to take it further. I'm not ready. But if I don't, I reckon he'll dump me for someone that will. It's awful because I really like him. But you shouldn't just do it because you want to keep the boy, should you?'

'That's the trouble when you go out with older boys,' I said. 'Wandering hands.'

'What should I do?'

'I've got just the thing,' I said, as Lucy looked hopeful. 'Have you got a photo of him?'

'Yes. We had some done in one of those photo booths.'

'OK,' I said. 'You do a spell. You cut the side of the photo with him on it and put it into the freezer and it will cool him down.'

Lucy laughed out loud. 'Oh come on. Get serious.'

At that moment, Nesta came back. 'What's so funny?'

'Nothing,' said Lucy, clamming up.

'Lucy was just telling me something one of the dogs did,' I said, trying to change the subject.

'Yeah, whatever,' said Nesta, sitting back down. 'Now what was I saying about movie stars and me?'

Lucy looked relieved that she hadn't caught on.

* * *

After I left the girls, I took the tube to Chalk Farm, where Dad lives now with his new wife Anna and their little boy Tom. Tom's gorgeous. He's only three. I like going to Dad's as it's so much more relaxed than Mum's house. I reckon she drove him out with all her constant cleaning and stuff.

Dad lectures in English at a university and the house is always cluttered with books and journals and papers. I feel at home there, as at least his house looks lived-in, unlike ours which is a cross between a hotel and a hospital clinic.

I was really heartbroken when Dad first left. I was seven at the time and for ages was convinced it was my fault and that I'd done something wrong.

One day Mum and Dad sat me down and explained that sometimes people can still like each other but can't live together any more and that's what had happened to them. Then they both said that no matter what happened, they both loved me and always would.

I felt better after that – that is until Angus moved in with my mum a couple of years later. I didn't like him at all at first. I asked if I could go and live with Dad, but he was living in a tiny flat at the time and there was no room for me.

Eventually, I decided that there was only one way to deal with Angus, and that's to pretend he's our lodger and be polite but nothing else. I mean, he's not my dad, is he? A lodger that just happens to sleep in the same bed as my mum, but I shut those kind of thoughts out of my head straight away. Yuk. I don't want to even go there.

I was looking forward to spending some time at Dad's and thought I'd spend the afternoon working on my songs.

'Excuse the mess,' said Dad as he opened the door, paint-brush in hand. 'We're doing up the study.'

'You've got paint all over your hair,' I laughed, looking at the white streaks in his normally dark hair. 'Did you actually manage to get *any* on the walls?'

'Hi, Izzie,' said Anna, appearing behind Dad. 'Welcome to the madhouse.'

Anna was one of Dad's students when they met five years ago. A mature student, he told me, in case I thought he was cradle-snatching. But mature or not, she's still twelve years younger than him, round and pretty with long auburn hair. She and Dad look right together. Dad always dresses in typical lecturer gear – jeans and leather jackets, looking most days like he's just got out of bed, and Anna still looks like a student, in jeans and sloppy jumpers. I don't think I've ever seen her in a skirt or dress.

I was glad when Dad met her, as I used to worry about him all alone in his small flat when I went to visit. I got on with her immediately and always found her easy to talk to. When they decided to get married I was the first to congratulate them, secretly hoping that they'd find a bigger house and then I could move in with them. But when they moved to this flat Tom came along and it's clear there's no room for me unless I sleep under the kitchen table.

I stepped over the various paint cans and boxes strewn in the hallway and made my way into their kitchen. Somehow I didn't think I was going to get any work done on my songs that afternoon.

'Izzie love . . .' Dad began.

'Yeees?' I said. I knew that tone of voice. He wanted something.

'First,' he said, 'I've got a book for you.'

I laughed to myself. Another for the box at the bottom of my cupboard, I thought. He was always giving me books to read – has since I was tiny. I got *War and Peace* for my ninth birthday. I don't think he's quite tuned into books for teenagers these days.

He handed me a book from the shelf in the kitchen. 'Dorothy Parker. I think you'll like her.'

'Thanks, Dad,' I said unconvincingly.

'No really,' said Anna, who was sympathetic to some of the heavy-going books he gave me to read. 'I really think you will.'

'OK, I'll take a look at it,' I said.

Then Dad smiled his 'I want something' smile. 'Would you do us the most enormous favour and take Tom out for a while? Anna and I want to finish the painting and it will be best if Tom's out of the way.'

'Sure, Dad,' I said as Tom paddled in and hugged my knees. 'No problem.'

'Izzie, you're an angel,' said Anna. 'I'll get his coat.'

'What, right now?' I asked. I'd hardly got there.

That's one of the minuses of having two sets of parents. You get two sets of chores.

I set off for the park with Tom and tried to distract him at the shops in Primrose Hill. I spotted an amazing black velvet dress in one of the displays and made a mental note to put it on my Christmas list.

Tom pulled on my coat. 'Swings,' he said, pointing to the end of the road.

'Shops,' I said hopefully, pointing to the windows which were bright with Christmas lights and tinsel. Sadly, Tom wasn't impressed. Like most males, he wasn't interested in shopping.

'OK, swings,' I said.

When we got to the play area there were a number of mothers there with their children and all the swings were full.

I sat on a park bench and wondered how best to keep a three-year-old entertained. Just at that moment, my mobile rang.

As I fished about in my bag to find my phone, I was

vaguely aware of someone walking towards us with a toddler. Whoever he was, he was on his mobile phone.

Just as I was about to answer my phone, the boy stopped in front of me. He gawped at the phone in his hand, then gawped at me.

'I've just called you!' said Mark.

My mouth dropped open. 'I don't believe it!'

'Neither do I. I call you, and here you are in front of me! It's so weird.'

My phone stopped ringing. 'Synchronicity,' I said.

'Right,' he said. 'What's that?'

I laughed. 'It's when something you're thinking about happens, or something to do with it does. I read about it. I'm not explaining it very well.'

'You're not a witch, are you?' asked Mark.

I thought about the love charm under my pillow. 'Might be,' I grinned.

After that we had the most brilliant time. I might not be a witch, I thought, but the afternoon was magic.

Mark had been landed with his little sister like I'd been landed with Tom. We spent hours playing on the swings and slides, joining in like kids ourselves. Then we had a go on the roundabouts. Mark was fantastic and knew loads of games that had Tom laughing and giggling.

We didn't have a lot of time to talk to each other but it

didn't matter, I thought, as I watched Mark rolling on the grass as his sister and Tom jumped all over him. Just being with him was fantastic.

After a few hours, my mobile rang.

'We thought you'd be back ages ago,' said Dad. 'Where on earth are you?'

I laughed. I wasn't on earth. I was somewhere up in the clouds.

# Chapter 7

# Big-mouth Nesta

'So are you going out with Mark now?' asked Lucy at break-time the following Monday.

'Not exactly, not yet,' I said. 'But he said he'd phone this week to arrange something. And this time I *know* he will because there he was, in front of me, phoning me. You should have been there. It was *amazing*. Like it was meant to be. And it was another day when my horoscope *said* that it was a good time for romance.'

Nesta looked doubtful. 'How do you know he really was phoning you? He could have seen you then felt guilty and *said* he was phoning you. I mean, you didn't check your phone right away, did you? Maybe he quickly rang you afterwards."

I shook my head. What was she on about? 'I didn't hear my phone go again. But I did leave my bag with Mark . . . '

Nesta's such a killjoy. I think she's jealous just because she's not in love with anyone at the moment.

Nesta shifted awkwardly. 'It's just that I tried to phone you on Saturday afternoon and no one picked up.'

Lucy saw my face drop. 'But it doesn't matter. You saw him. That's what matters.'

It was too late. The rosy glow I'd been feeling turned into a black cloud. As the bell rang, I turned to go back into class. I wasn't going to speak to Nesta any more. Now she'd ruined everything.

'Oh Izzie,' said Nesta, catching up with me. 'I'm sorry. I didn't mean to . . . '

'You and your big mouth,' said Lucy to Nesta. 'Now you've put your foot in it.'


After school each night, I went home alone. I felt such an idiot. Pathetic. I couldn't face going back to Lucy's with her and Nesta like normal. I felt mad at Nesta, even though she might have been right. And I didn't want them being all nice and feeling sorry for me. I didn't know what to think, and wanted some time on my own to sort my head out. I felt really confused.

Each night, I had to walk past the pizza shop on my way home. I could really do with one of those right now, I thought – deep pan, four cheese, and I wouldn't care if it all went straight to my bum. It's hard staying healthy at times like this when I've been feeling so mixed up. I was beginning to think what does it matter? So I am what I eat. A limp lettuce? Pooh.

Every evening seemed *soo loooong*, like each minute was eternal as I sat in my room, willing the phone to ring. And it didn't. I wished I had his number so I could call him but I didn't even know his last name.

One night I decided to distract myself by reading my Feng Shui book: *Each room is divided into different areas, each area representing a different part of your life: creativity, wealth, knowledge, family, friends, relationships. Each area falls in a positive or negative space depending on whether the room faces north, south, east or west.*

I got my compass out and did some calculations. That's what was wrong, I realised. I'd got my wastepaper bin in my relationship corner! *Disastrous*. It meant I was putting rubbish into my relationships. Durrh. No wonder Mark hadn't phoned.

I rearranged my room according to the book then started on the bathroom.

'What on earth are you doing?' said Angus, finding me kneeling in the corner trying to Blu-Tack the rose quartz crystal I bought for Mum for Christmas to the waste-pipe.

'Nothing,' I said.

'Nothing,' he said, then stood hovering at the doorway.

He looked as though he wanted to say something but eventually just shrugged. 'OK, suit yourself.'

I wasn't going to waste my breath explaining that in the bathroom, our loo was in the relationship corner in a negative zone so we were flushing all the good relationship energy away. The book said a crystal on the plumbing would help direct the energy back up again. But Angus would never understand that. All he understands is the *Financial Times* and insurance policies.

Another night, for want of anything else to do – or eat – (Mum *still* hadn't got the message about buying more healthy stuff) I munched my way through half a packet of choc chip cookies. Before I ate the other half, I decided to use my time more positively and do an exercise DVD. It's called *Bums, Tums and Thighs*, and promises you a whole new body in four weeks.

What it doesn't tell you is that the next day, you'll be so stiff you probably won't be able to walk.

Another night and there was still *nothing* to do. I'd done my homework and there was nothing on the TV so I had a quick look at the book Dad gave me about Dorothy Parker. She sounded pretty cool. She was a writer who lived in New York around the 1920s and it sounded like she had a rotten time with some of her boyfriends, but she managed to be really funny about it. She used to meet up with other writers of the day at a round table in a place called the Alonquin Hotel and would have them all rolling in the aisles with her poems and sayings about love going wrong and stuff. It sounded like a brilliant time and I thought I'd like to be like her when I grow up. We've got a round table downstairs in our dining-room so Nesta, Lucy and me could have meetings like she did. There was a photo of her at the back of the book and it gave me an idea.

I went into the kitchen, got the scissors, then went into the bathroom, the one room in this house where I could lock the door. My hair is all one length and I thought it might look more interesting if I cut a fringe like Dorothy Parker's. I pulled a short section up at the front and snip, off it came. I combed it out and it looked pretty good. Except it was a bit uneven on one side. So I snipped a bit more off. Oops, a bit too much. I'd better even it out. Oops. OOOOPS. Oh *no*. Now *that* was uneven. I chopped off a bit more then stood back to look at my reflection. Tears filled my eyes. I'd managed to cut it down to a stubble. I tried to comb it under the long bits. But it kept sticking out again.

Oh God, what had I done? Stupid. Stupid. I'd just ruined my hair. Now I knew how Lucy had felt when she had a bad haircut earlier that term. What on earth had possessed me? Now I couldn't go out. It'd takes weeks to grow back. It was all Mark's fault. If he had phoned none of it would have happened. Could life get any worse? I could hardly walk from doing all those exercises and now I looked like a mad person. All because of a boy. I was seriously beginning to wonder if they're worth the trouble.

*And* I was getting a huge spot. On the end of my *nose*.

'Izzie, what are you doing in there?' said Mum's voice on the other side of the door. 'You've been in there ages.'

There was nothing else for it. She was bound to see sooner or later. I opened the door and waited for the telling off. I didn't care. I felt numb. Sometimes I can be *so* stupid.

'Oh Izzie,' said Mum. 'What have you done?'

'Only ruined my hair!' I wailed. 'Now I can never go out again.'

She gently pushed me back into the bathroom and took a closer look. 'Got a bit carried away, didn't you?'

I nodded miserably. 'Aren't you going to yell at me?'

Mum shook her head. 'Do you want me to see if I can fix it?'

'No, I don't think so.'

Mum pulled a bit more hair over my face. 'I think I could. If I cut a bit more fringe then cut into it, then you wouldn't see the short bits underneath. Want to give it a go?'

Mum used to cut my hair when I was little. My gran used to be a hairdresser and Mum had picked up the basics from her so I knew I could trust her not to make it any worse.

'OK.' I quickly showed her the photo of Dorothy Parker

at the back of my book. 'I was trying to cut a fringe like hers.'

'Dorothy Parker! I thought most girls your age wanted to look like those girls in The Saturdays?'

'Not me.'

'That's my Izzie.' Mum smiled at me. 'Always has to be different.'

'Will you get me a wig for Christmas if it doesn't work out?'

'Sure,' laughed Mum. 'But I don't think it will come to that. OK. Wet it a bit then it will cut better.'

I did as I was told and Mum carefully snipped a bit more fringe then began to cut into it. 'It's looking better already. And I'll take some off the length so it doesn't look top-heavy.'

'Whatever,' I said.

She finished cutting and combing and then took me into her bedroom, got the hairdryer out and blew it dry.

'Can I look now?' I asked.

Mum nodded and I went and stood in front of her mirror. I was shocked. It looked really good. Just past my shoulders. More modern. And if I pushed it back it fell in a really nice layer.

'Not bad, eh?' said Mum, looking pleased with herself.

'Mum, you're a genius,' I said and hugged her.

Now Mark just had to phone. He'd be bound to fancy me more with my new haircut.

★ ★ ★

At school the next day, Lucy and Nesta seemed agitated about something. In fact, I don't think Nesta even noticed my hair until Lucy said she liked it.

Nesta cornered me in the corridor at lunch-time. 'Izzie, I know I put my foot in it the other day and I think we need to clear the air. Plus we have to talk about Lucy and Tony. I . . .'

Then Lucy came round the corner and Nesta clammed up.

Then Nesta went to get a drink from the machine in the hall, and Lucy started up. 'Izzie, I need to talk to you.'

'About Tony?' I said.

'Yes. No. Yeah. About Tony but about you as well. I've hardly seen you lately and . . .'

Then *she* clammed up when Nesta came back.

'What's going on?' said Nesta, eyeing us suspiciously.

Then *I* clammed up. Honestly. It's supposed to be *me* who's going slowly bonkers. Now they're acting all weird and I've lost track of who's not talking to who about what and why. I don't know what Lucy's problem is – at least she *knows* Tony likes her. All I know is Mark still hasn't called and I don't know where I stand with him at all.

As we went back into class for the afternoon, I could see Lucy was looking miserable and I wondered if it was my fault. I suppose I have been a bit wrapped up in myself lately. What a mess.

When I got home on Friday night, *finally*, my mobile rang.

Let it be Mark, let it be Mark, I prayed as I leaped to answer it.

But it was only Lucy.

'Izzie, it's me,' she said. 'If you're mad at Nesta, why aren't you speaking to me?'

'I *am* speaking to you, Lucy. And Nesta. It's just I feel like being on my own lately,' I said.

'Well I miss you,' she said. 'Has Mark phoned?'

'Not yet. But I don't care any more,' I lied.

'Maybe Mercury's gone retrograde again?' she said.

'Nah. I've checked. It's supposed to be a good week for me according to my horoscope. In fact, the print-out I've just done says I'll hear from someone I want to.'

'*Meeee,*' said Lucy. 'That's me. One of your best mates. Remember?'

'Yeah,' I said unconvincingly.

'I *am* sorry he's not phoned,' said Lucy. 'But I think you're letting it get to you.'

'No I'm not,' I said. 'I'm perfectly cool with it all.'

'Then come over for a bit. We could watch the soaps or a DVD.'

'Can't,' I said. 'I'm having an early night.'

I could hear Lucy sigh at the other end. 'OK. I'll call Nesta and see if *she* wants to come over.'

I felt a bit rotten after I put the phone down, and hoped that Lucy would understand.

I waited in all night. But the phone stayed silent.

On Saturday morning I checked my horoscope and it said it was a good day for confrontations so I decided I'd go to the Lock and if Mark was there, I'd have it out with him. Ask him why he hadn't called this week and if he really was phoning me last week when we met.

Unfortunately Big-Mouth phoned just as I was ready to leave.

'I'm so sorry about Monday, Izzie,' said Nesta. 'I can't bear it when you're mad with me. Come to Hampstead. Lucy and I both want to see you. We think you need a break from thinking about Mark.'

'Can't,' I said. 'Busy.'

Nesta went quiet on the other end of the phone. 'I hope you're not thinking of going to the Lock.'

'No. Anyway, why?' I asked.

'Because you *mustn't*,' said Nesta. 'You *know* boys don't like it if you chase them or get heavy. They don't like hassle, especially when it's early days.'

'What makes you think I'm going to get heavy with him?'

Nesta paused at the other end of the phone. 'Well, you have been kind of intense lately, even with me and Lucy.'

'No I haven't.'

'OK,' Nesta sighed. 'But you haven't been your usual self. You might think I don't understand but I do. And I can see that Mark has really got to you. Trust me, Iz. It's really not a good idea to go to the Lock. You need to chill out a bit before you see him again.'

'Fine,' I said.

'Fine,' said Nesta.

Then I hung up. I wasn't going to listen to her. Killjoy.

I made my way to the Lock, praying that Mark was working that day. I went over and over in my head what I planned to say but Nesta had got me worried. I didn't want to be 'heavy' but I really wanted to know where I stood. We'd had such a good time last week. I couldn't have imagined it. Oh, I *wished* I could feel normal again.

I was feeling really nervous as I went into the market. Was this a good idea? Should I turn back now?

'Izzie!' called Mark. He was there at the stall and had seen me coming up the stairs.

'Oh, hi,' I said, forcing my voice to sound casual. 'I forgot you worked here.'

He looked at me strangely. 'Really?' he said. He looked hurt.

We both stood there looking awkward. All my carefully prepared words deserted me. I didn't know *what* to say.

'Er, better be going then . . . ' I said finally.

'Oh.' He looked disappointed. 'I was just going to take a break. Can't you stay a mo? We could get a cappuccino.'

I felt as if someone had poured concrete in my brain and I'd turned to stone. I was torn. Should I go, should I stay? Perhaps he'd explain. Perhaps I could ask my questions. Either way, I wanted to know what he had to say.

'OK,' I said.

We made our way downstairs and Mark bought two cappuccinos at a take-away stall.

'Sugar?' he asked.

I shook my head. Perhaps this wasn't the best time to say I wasn't drinking coffee. He might think I was a weirdo.

We sat by the canal sipping our drinks. Lovely. Bliss. Oh I'd forgotten how nice and creamy and frothy these could be. Perhaps I could do my healthy eating but have the occasional treat. Balance, I told myself, that's what it's all about.

'Er, Mark . . . ' I began.

'Yeah,' he smiled back at me.

'You know when you said you'd phone me . . .'

'Oh yeah. I was going to tell you. My mobile got nicked. I was going to phone you.'

Suddenly he looked uncomfortable. Had I gone too far? But if his mobile had been stolen maybe that explained it. Not really, I thought. There are other phones. I decided to jump right in. I didn't want to spend another week agonising over whether he was interested or playing games. I had nothing to lose.

'You know when we saw each other last Saturday and you were phoning me?'

'Yeah,' he smiled and put his hand over mine on the table. 'That was amazing, wasn't it? Synchronicity, like you said.'

A lovely tingling feeling went right through me. I cast about in my head for how I could ask him without sounding like I didn't trust him.

'Was that your dad who answered the phone?' said Mark, interrupting my confusion.

'What do you mean? My dad?'

'When I phoned you.'

I was more confused than ever. 'What do you mean?'

'When I saw you, remember? I'd just called you when there you were in front of me.'

'Yeah. And I was just about to pick up.'

'Yeah. But I wasn't phoning your mobile. There were two numbers on your card. I called the first one and some bloke answered.'

He must have phoned my home number. And *Angus*. Angus must have picked up.

'So you didn't phone me on my mobile? You called my *house*.'

'Yeah, was that your dad? He sounded very posh.'

'No,' I said. 'It must have been the lodger that picked up.'

'Anyway,' said Mark, playing with my fingers, 'there you were in front of me.'

Suddenly the rosy glow came back. Nesta had been right. It must have been her on my mobile and that's why she said no one picked up. But he had phoned. Hurrah. It was going to be all right after all.


When I got home later that day I stormed into the kitchen to find Angus. He was sitting with my mum at the table, drinking a cup of tea.

'Hi, Izzie,' they chorused.

'Why didn't you tell me someone called last Saturday?' I demanded, turning to Angus.

Angus looked startled. 'What? When? What are you talking about?'

'Don't you even remember?' I said. 'It's *really* important.'

Angus scratched his head. 'When did you say?'

'Last Saturday?' I had to know if Mark was telling the truth.

'I don't know. Did someone leave a message and I forgot to pass it on? Let me think.'

'They might not have left a message. A boy. A boy's voice.'

Mum and Angus gave each other a knowing look.

'Oh yes, I think the phone did go at some point,' said Angus. 'But no one was on the other end. I presumed it was a wrong number.'

I wanted to kill him. 'You should have *told* me!' I cried.

'Izzie, don't speak to Angus like that. He wasn't to know it wasn't a wrong number, especially if no one even spoke! He's not psychic.'

Tears pricked the back of my eyes. 'You don't understand, do you?' I turned back to Angus. 'You almost ruined *everything*.'

'Sit down and have some lunch with us, Izzie,' said Mum softly. 'Tell us what you've been up to.'

'You wouldn't understand!' I wailed. 'And anyway, there's never anything I can eat in this house. Nobody cares about me . . .'

Mum's expression clouded. 'I'm getting *really* tired of your selfish attitude, Isobel. Go to your room. And don't come down until you're ready to apologise.'

I stormed out and slammed the door. Go to your room. That's all I ever heard these days. I couldn't do anything right. Mums. I give up.

# SONG FOR MUM
## by Izzie Foster

Hey Mum, I want you to know,
So sit down and listen,
No please don't go.
Things are different since you were a girl,
Pressures today put my head in a whirl.
Life's moving faster, we're all in the race
That's accelerated to a damaging pace.
Sometimes it's too much to bear,
So when I come home and seem in despair
Don't ask what's wrong, leave me alone.

I'm good, I'm bad,
You're nice, you're mad.
I love, I hate,
But it's never too late
To say sorry.

It's tough to say about your man,
So please forgive me if I'm not a fan
But he's not my dad and that's a fact.
Yes I know, I know I'm lacking tact,
Blame my ignorance, my stupid youth.
You always said to speak the truth.
I share your guilt and feel your pain,
I just hide mine in a secret place.

# Chapter 8

# Mobile Madness

I don't *believe* what's just happened.

When I left Mark on Saturday, my plan to ask him for his number went out of the window as once again, he promised to call me. I told him not to phone my home number as Mum and the lodger were hopeless at passing on messages. So he said he'd call on my mobile. Simple.

Or so I thought.

I checked my weekly horoscope and it said a slow start to the week but things would liven up around Thursday when Pluto was square to Mars, causing some confusion. Hah! Understatement.

On Thursday evening, Mum took me to Lucy's house to have my guitar lesson with Lucy's dad. She said she'd wait for me and as she got settled with a magazine in the kitchen, Mr L and I went through to the sitting-room. We'd just got started on some chord exercises when my mobile rang.

'Turn that off for the lesson,' said Mr L.

'Can I please take this call, just this one?' I begged. It might be Mark and I didn't want to miss him.

'Well, just this one,' said Mr L. 'Then I want your full concentration.'

'Izzie, it's me,' said Nesta's croaky voice. 'I really need to talk to you.'

'Can't at the moment,' I said. 'I'm in the middle of a guitar lesson. Speak later.'

I was feeling a bit rotten about Nesta. She'd been off with flu all week and I hadn't even called her. And I knew she hadn't meant to be mean about Mark and I *knew* I owed her an apology but I wanted to pick my time. Not when Mr L was listening in.

I put my mobile on the table where I could see it.

'Off,' said Mr L. 'Switch it *off* for the lesson.'

'Ohhh, do I have to?'

'You do. I know what you girls are like on your phones and I've got another pupil straight after you so I don't want us wasting time.'

I could see he meant it so, reluctantly, I switched the phone off and turned my mind to the guitar.

'You're getting better,' said Mr L at the end of our hour. 'Now did you bring me some of your songs to look at? Next time, we could start putting them to music.'

'Er, yes, no,' I squirmed.

'Er, yes, no. Did you or didn't you?'

I had brought my lyrics with me but I didn't want to show them. Not since that lesson when everyone laughed at my rap song.

'I did bring them,' I said. 'But I don't want to show them.'

'Ah, a songwriter who doesn't want anyone to hear her songs?'

'I read a few lines of one of them in class and everyone laughed,' I said.

Mr L looked at me kindly. 'It's hard, Izzie, when you do anything creatively. There will always be people who like what you do and those who don't. You mustn't take it personally. But if you're going to succeed, and I'm sure you will, you've got to be ready to take constructive criticism. Don't be afraid to stick your neck out. Just be careful who you show your work to in the beginning. Some people will criticise because they're jealous but others can give you feedback that you can learn from.'

'Well, will you read them when I'm not here? Then I don't have to see your face if you don't like them.'

Mr L laughed. 'Sure. Leave them on top of the piano there. You needn't be afraid, I'm sure I *will* like them.'

'Well promise you won't show them to anyone. Promise, not Lal or Steve or even Lucy. I've never shown them to anyone.'

'Promise.'

As I left the room, I noticed my mum chatting to a boy in the kitchen. She looked up as she saw us coming in.

'Er, can I have a word?' she said to Mr L.

'Sure,' he said.

'In private,' she said and went off into the living-room with him. What's all that about? I thought.

I looked across at the boy. He looked familiar. 'Hey, don't I know you?' I asked.

The boy nodded and smiled. 'Yeah, Ben. From your sister's wedding.'

'Stepsister,' I corrected.

He looked really different from the way he'd looked at the wedding, cute almost, and in the same school uniform as Lucy's brothers.

'You go to the same school as Lal and Steve?'

'Yeah,' he said. 'That's how I heard about the lessons.'

'Where are they all? Lucy and Steve and Lal?'

'Gone to get pizza, I think,' he said.

'So you're the next pupil?'

'Yeah,' he said.

At that moment, Mum came back out. 'Ready? she asked.

'Who was that?' she asked as we drove away.

'No one,' I said. 'He was at the wedding playing those awful songs.'

'I *thought* I recognised him,' said Mum. 'Of course, he's

Jeremy's younger brother. He was rather good on the piano, wasn't he?'

'Oh Mum, the music he played was totally naff. I'm surprised he's bothering to have lessons. He clearly hasn't a clue about decent music.'

'What were you talking about?' she asked.

'Nothing,' I replied. 'Why, what were you talking to Mr L about?'

Mum got a really cheeky look on her face. 'Oh nothing,' she mimicked then we both burst out laughing.

It was only when we got home that I realised I'd left my mobile on the table at Lucy's. And it was switched off.

'I *have* to go back,' I said to Mum. 'I've left my mobile.'

'You can live without it for one night,' said Mum. 'Call Lucy and ask her to take it into school in the morning.'

I went to the phone to call Lucy and saw that the answering machine was flashing two messages.

I pressed the playback button.

'Hi, it's Mark,' said the first message. 'I tried calling your mobile but it's switched off so I thought I'd try your home number. Anyway, you're not there either so I'll try your mobile again later.'

'Oh *no*,' I groaned.

Then there was a beep and a message from Angus for Mum saying he was working late. Oh pants. Now I couldn't do 1471 to get Mark's number as Angus had called in between and got in the way. *Again.*

I quickly called Lucy, explained the situation and asked her to check if anyone had rung.

A few minutes later, she came back to the phone. 'Only a message from Nesta about five minutes ago.'

'Oh *no*,' I said. 'Mark said he'd try and call. Now I can't do 1471 on that phone *either* as Nesta's will be the last number. Promise you'll answer it if it goes again?'

'Course I will,' she said. 'And have you phoned Nesta?'

'Not yet. Why?'

'She really wants to talk to you,' said Lucy.

Oh dear. She was mad at me. I'd better phone soon and make it up with her. But first, I had to get my mobile back.

I went into the sitting-room where Mum had settled on the sofa in front of the TV with a glass of wine.

'Mum. Please will you take me back to Lucy's to get my mobile?'

'Izzie. It's eight o'clock.'

'It'll only take twenty minutes.'

She sighed. Never a good sign. 'I've had a long day at work, I took you to your music lesson, I waited for you and I'm *not* going back there now. We have a phone here.'

'Well I'll go on the bus.'

'You will not, not on your own at this time of night.'

'Then I'll get a taxi.'

'Izzie. Watch my lips. N. O. *No*. Anyway, who was that boy on the answering machine?'

'No one.'

'Well what did he want?'

'Nothing,' I said.

This time, neither of us laughed.

# Chapter 9

# Murphy's Law

At school on Friday, things really came to a head.

I know Mum's mad at me. Nothing unusual there. But now Lucy is too.

'Have you called Nesta yet?' she said when she handed over my mobile phone in the break.

'Not yet,' I said. 'I did mean to . . . but . . . '

'But *what*?' said Lucy crossly. 'She's phoned you a few times. And she's not well. What's the excuse this time? Mercury gone retrograde again so you can't pick up a phone?'

I was stunned. This wasn't like Lucy. She was all stiff and looked really upset.

'I will phone her. I've had a lot going on. And *actually*, it's not Mercury, it's Pluto, it's going through a really intense phase in my chart and . . . '

'Tell me about it,' said Lucy, looking skywards. 'Not only

Pluto. *You*, Izzie. You're so . . . so serious about everything these days. And you can't keep blaming the stars. In fact, I'm getting sick of you using your stupid horoscope as an excuse for everything anyone does, doesn't do or thinks. You know what? You're no fun any more. *And* you've been neglecting me. And Nesta. You're not the only one going through stuff. But lately it's all been about you. And Mark. And if he's phoned or not. And Mercury or Venus . . .'

She broke off. She looked near to tears. She turned away but I went and stood in front of her and put my hand on her arm.

'Oh don't cry, Lucy. You're right. I'm sorry. I've been a pain, haven't I?'

'Yes. You *have*.'

'Look, I'll phone Nesta this instant,' I said and began dialling Nesta's number. 'And I'll make it up to you. Honest I will. Lucy. Lucy? Still mates? Please?'

Lucy sighed. 'Course,' she said. 'Still mates. Just lighten up a bit, will you?'

At that moment the bell went for class.

'I'll phone Nesta at lunch. I will. I *will*. Promise.'

'You better had,' said Lucy and punched my arm.

But at least she was smiling.


When I got home that evening, I had a good think about everything Lucy had said. I knew she was right. I had lost myself somewhere along the way in the last few weeks. And to tell the truth, I was beginning to get tired of staying in waiting for the phone and going slowly mental. I'd done everything I could think of to keep myself occupied. I'd colour co-ordinated my wardrobe, I'd tidied all my books and CDs, I'd done all my homework, painted my nails, conditioned my hair, written my Christmas cards. I realised that I had to stop waiting around for Mark to phone, it was ridiculous. I had to get myself a life again. I'd been neglecting my friends. And I was starting to miss them.

When Lucy phoned and asked if I wanted to go to Nesta's, I didn't think twice.

'See you there at seven,' I said.


'I'm not infectious any more,' said Nesta as Lucy and I sat as far away as we could from her in their sitting-room. 'In fact, Mum says I can go out again tomorrow. Hurrah.'

Lucy laughed, then went and plonked herself on the floor by the sofa where Nesta was lying like the Queen of Sheba, covered in a huge duvet and surrounded by boxes of tissues and Lemsips.

I'd phoned Nesta at lunch-time as promised and, before she could say anything, I apologised for being a total pain. We talked for about an hour and I didn't even get in a state about Mark maybe trying to get through. She was great about everything and said she really values me as a friend. I felt really close to her. She said she was sorry for putting the damper on my day in the park with Mark and I said I'd been a complete prat. She agreed. We had a laugh and here we were like nothing ever happened.

'How do you handle it, Lucy?' I asked. 'If Tony doesn't phone?'

'Easy,' said Nesta. 'I stand over him to make sure he does. I told him from the start that he'd better not mess her around and he knows better than to get me mad.'

Lucy and I laughed. We both knew what Nesta could be like when she turned into Scary Girl mode. Not to be argued with.

'Anyway,' I said, joining Lucy on the floor. 'I've had enough of boys. Too much trouble. Up. Down. Happy. Depressed. I can't take it any more. I was OK before I met Mark. And I've been mental ever since.'

'Did he call this evening?' asked Lucy.

'What do you think?'

'Maybe?' said Lucy.

'Nah,' I said. 'And I've had enough. *Enough*. I don't know what game he's playing but I don't want to join in. First he says he had a mad week, then, last Saturday, he says his mobile was nicked . . . '

Nesta's face dropped.

'What?' I asked. 'What is it?'

'Nothing,' she said. But I could tell that there was something she wasn't saying. And I could tell Lucy knew whatever it was as she looked really worried too.

'Nesta. Spill.'

She shook her head. 'No, honestly, nothing. It doesn't matter.'

We sat awkwardly for a few minutes.

'Nesta, you *have* to tell me. I *know* you know something. If you don't tell me I will imagine the worst possible thing in the world.'

'Like what?' she asked.

'Er, like secretly you've been dating Mark all this time?'

She laughed. 'No, it's not *that* bad. Besides, you know I wouldn't do that.'

'So what, then?'

She shifted uncomfortably. 'Well, promise you won't stop speaking to me again.'

'Promise,' I said, starting to feel pretty uncomfortable myself. 'Look, I know I've been a useless mate lately but I promise I won't go funny, whatever you tell me.'

I *had* to know. There's *nothing* I hate more than when someone says they know something, then won't tell you.

'Well, last Saturday, remember you wouldn't come out with us to the Hollywood Bowl?'

'Yes,' I nodded.

'Well, we saw Mark there.'

'Really?'

'Yeah. He was with a bunch of mates.'

'Well that's not so bad. I mean, we didn't have a date or anything.'

'Yeah. But he was posing about. On his mobile phone.'

'Oh,' I said. 'The creep. Why didn't he just say he'd forgotten to ring or something? Why come up with a whole story about his phone being nicked?'

'Boys do that when they feel confronted,' said Lucy. 'Believe me, I know, with two stupid brothers. Rather than tell the truth they'll make up some daft story so they don't look bad.'

'Well that's it, then,' I said. 'No more boys. No matter how cute.'

'Until you meet the next one you like,' said Nesta.

'No,' I said. I really meant it this time. 'Boys are bad for your mental health.'

'Some are OK,' said Nesta. 'They don't all mess you around. But friends are best. It's not worth losing your friends over any boy.'

'Absolutely,' I agreed. 'I mean, boys will come and go. But we'll always be friends and be there for each other. Won't we? Let's make a pact that we'll never ever let a boy come between us again.'

'Yeah,' said Nesta. 'And we'll always tell the truth to each other, no matter how much we think it might hurt.'

'Yeah,' said Lucy. 'A pact. If you can't trust your mates, then who can you trust?'

I felt happier than I had for weeks. Sane again. It felt good to be back with my pals. Easy company. Uncomplicated.

'To no boys,' I said.

Lucy and Nesta looked doubtful.

'How about to friends?' said Nesta.

'OK,' I said. 'To friends.'


When I got home later that night, Mum called me into the sitting-room. She was curled up on the sofa reading a vegetarian recipe book and Angus was at the desk in the bay window, looking at some photographs in an album. Oh no, I thought. *Please* don't let those be the wedding pictures come back. That was an episode I was hoping had been forgiven and forgotten.

'What are you reading a vegetarian recipe book for?' I said, edging out of the room just in case the photos were from the wedding and it all blew up again.

'Just looking at a few recipes for Christmas dinner,' said Mum. 'We can't have you eating nothing but sprouts. How does a nut roast sound?'

'Great,' I said. What was going on? She didn't seem too mad. Perhaps it wasn't Amelia's wedding album.

'Want to see yourself as bridesmaid, Izzie?' asked Angus.

I looked nervously at Mum, thinking, Oh-oh, here we go.

But she didn't even look up from her book.

I went to look over Angus's shoulder. 'Wow!' I said. 'They look fantastic.'

Angus turned and smiled. 'Yes. Good solution, eh?'

'Yeah,' I said, breathing a sigh of relief. 'Excellent solution.'

He'd had the photos done in black and white. In the few photos I was in, I looked completely normal. No wonder Mum was sitting there so cool about it all. In black and white, no one need ever know her mad daughter had green hair on the day.

'Some boy called when you were out,' said Mum. 'Mark. He said he'd phone back.'

'Oh *no*,' I said. 'Murphy's Law.'

Mum looked at me quizzically. 'Oh no? I thought he was the one that all the fuss was about?'

I sighed. 'He was. But I just decided I'm through with boys.'

Mum and Angus laughed.

'I can't keep up, Izzie,' said Mum.

'Neither can I,' I said. 'I'm going to bed.'


As I went up the stairs, I had an idea.

'Has anyone called since?'

'No,' said Mum. 'I don't think so.'

Great! I went into the hall and dialled 1471.

I scribbled down the number then went up to my room.

At last! I thought. Now I could call him if I wanted.
But I was through with boys. Wasn't I?

# STAYING TOGETHER
## by Izzie Foster

Hey there, don't you know that boys just come and boys
    just go,
But friends stay together for ever and ever.
Hey there, follow the noise and you'll soon find a gang
    of boys.

Had enough of football chants?
Smelly trainers, mindless rants?
Boys are stupid, boys are vain,
A dozen boys just share one brain.
No boys!

Yes, girlfriend, it's the truth, we're not going to waste our
    youth.
Friends stay together for ever and ever.
We're too pretty, we're too smart
    to let any boyfriend break us apart.

Boys are stupid, boys are vain,
A dozen boys just share one brain.
No boys!

# Chapter 10

# Cosmic Kisses

'I have a date,' I said to Lucy on the phone the following morning. 'A proper date. With Mark.'

He'd phoned back five minutes after I got home from Nesta's, so I hadn't had to think about whether to phone him or not.

'We're going to hang out this afternoon. Don't be mad with me.'

'I'm not mad with you,' she said. 'But I thought you were through with boys.'

'I know, I *know*. But a girl can change her mind, can't she?'

Talking about changing her mind, I must have tried on every outfit in my wardrobe. Nothing looked right. I wanted to look my best but didn't want to look like I'd made too much effort.

By twelve o'clock I had every item I owned out on the bed and I was meeting Mark in an hour. Help.

'Having a clear-out?' asked Mum, coming into my bedroom and surveying the mess everywhere.

'*Mum,*' I said. 'You didn't knock.'

Mum raised her eyes to the ceiling. 'You never used to mind, Izzie.'

'Well I do now. I'm fourteen.'

'Anyway,' said Mum, ignoring me. 'What are you doing?'

'*Trying* to get dressed. But I've got nothing to wear.'

Mum looked at the heaps of clothes piled on the bed. 'Nothing to wear?' she laughed. 'There's loads of clothes here. Anyway, what's the occasion?'

I shrugged. I didn't want to tell her I was going out with Mark as she'd want to know everything. Who he was. What school he went to. Then she'd be inviting him round to give him the once-over. No thanks.

'I'm going to the Hollywood Bowl,' I said. She didn't need to know who with. But she had a silly grin on her face. I think she knew.

'Then just wear your jeans.'

'My bum looks big in them.'

'Then wear a skirt.'

'I can't decide,' I sighed, looking pointedly at my watch.

'OK. OK. I know when I'm not wanted,' Mum said, turning to leave. 'And Izzie?'

'Yes?' Please don't let her ask too many questions, I prayed.

'Have a good time,' she winked.

Sometimes I don't get parents.

In the end, I grabbed my black sweater, my black jeans and black fitted blazer. Black and mysterious, that's me.

The weather looked freezing outside so I added a red scarf and gloves, then a bit of lippie, a bit of kohl, a spray of Mum's Chanel No. 19 and I was out the door.


Mark was waiting for me outside Café Original when I got to North Finchley. I was glad I hadn't dressed up too much as besides his jacket, he had on a navy jumper, jeans and trainers. I tried my best to look cool as I walked towards him but my heart was beating madly. He looked gorgeous.

Gorgeous and waiting for me.

Gorgeous, waiting for me and waving.

My breath felt tight in my chest as I waved back.

'Hi,' he said, taking my hand and leading me into the café. 'Let's go and get a drink to warm us up.'

As we walked into the café all my anxieties from the last few weeks melted away. What did any of it matter now? I could see a few girls eyeing him up as we got drinks and took our seats.

Ha ha, I thought, he's with me. On a date. With *me*.

We spent the next few hours jibber-jabbering about everything. I found out he lives in Primrose Hill not far from

Dad. He goes to school there as well and, most excellent, it's one of the five local schools invited to our end-of-term prom. He's seventeen and a Libra (which is an air sign like me, so we're really compatible). His favourite films are *Batman Begins, Superbad* and *Inception* (which is my favourite film). He's got one older brother and a younger sister. Best subjects are Maths and Biology and he wants to be a doctor when he grows up.

We'd just ordered two blueberry muffins (my weekend treat) and got on to our favourite foods, when a phone rang. He reached into his pocket and pulled out his mobile.

After he'd finished his call, he grinned at me. 'Sorry about that. One of my mates, I'm seeing him later,' he said.

I put on my most innocent look. 'I thought you said your phone had been nicked.'

He shifted awkwardly and I could have sworn he blushed a bit. 'Oh yeah,' he said. 'That. My dad got me a new one yesterday.'

We ate our muffins in silence then he looked right into my eyes and did a kind of slow smile. Then he stared at my mouth for a moment and my insides went all tingly.

'Shall we go and have a walk before we go home?' he asked.

Suddenly I felt really nervous. It was our first date. Would he want to kiss me? I'd only ever kissed two other boys and neither of them were important. One boy when I was a kid and then some creepoid last year who had a nasty case of wandering hands. It was horrible and he poked his tongue in my mouth. All I could think was wet fish, wet fish! Sloppy, slimy. Blaghh.

This time it would be for real.

I tried to remember what Nesta's brother had told us about kissing. Tony fancies himself as the Master Snogger and one time, before he was going out with Lucy, he offered to show me how it was done. I laughed at him but now I wished I'd taken him up on it. I mean, how do you know if you're a good kisser? I cast my mind back and desperately tried to remember what his snogging tips were. I should have asked Lucy or Nesta before I came out. I know, I thought, I'll phone them.

'Sure, a walk sounds good,' I said. 'But just got to go to the ladies'. Won't be a mo.'

I dashed into the ladies', waited until all the cubicles were empty, then dialled Lucy's number.

'Lucy,' I said. 'I'm with Mark. What do I do if he wants to kiss me?'

Lucy laughed. 'Durrh. Snog him back, dummy.'

'But how?' I wailed. 'I'm really worried I'll be useless at it and he'll never want to see me again.'

'Relax,' said Lucy. 'Just take your lead from him.'

'What if he puts his tongue in my mouth? What do I do?'

'Just do what feels natural,' said Lucy.

'Thanks,' I said, feeling none the wiser. I phoned Nesta for a second opinion.

'Fresh breath,' she said. 'V. important. Otherwise, keep the pressure varied. Soft, medium, hard, and run your fingers through his hair. Boys like that.'

'What do I do with my tongue?'

'Stick it up his nostril,' she giggled.

'Ergh, *Nesta*!'

'Izzie, relax. You'll be fine. Ring me later with all the details.'

Thanks for nothing, Nesta, I thought as I switched off my phone. Just because she's snogged loads of boys she thinks it's really funny.

I rooted round in my bag and found some chewing gum then put on some lipstick. Oh. Was that a good idea? If he kissed me he'd get it all over him. Maybe I should wipe it off again? God, it was so complicated. We ought to have lessons in this sort of thing at school instead of all that stuff we never needed about how many crops are grown in some remote country I'd never heard of.

I rubbed my lipstick into my lips so that it wasn't too shiny then went back out to meet him. Gulp! He was chewing gum as well. Snogging was definitely on the cards. I pushed my gum behind my teeth so he wouldn't see I was chewing as well. I didn't want him to think I was expecting it or anything.

When we got outside, we had a look at what was on at the movies then it started raining so we made a dash for the bus stop. We were the only people there and I wondered if he was going to make a move. Or should I? Or would that seem forward? I was shivering like mad though I wasn't sure if that was from the cold or nerves.

After an agonising two minutes, Mark stepped forward and put his arms round me. He felt gorgeous, all warm, solid and safe.

'Freezing, isn't it?' he said. 'Let's keep each other warm.'

I went rigid. This is it, I thought. Get ready to pucker.

He leaned his face towards me and I moved towards him and we banged noses.

'Oops,' he laughed. Then he leaned in again and kissed me.

At first it was a shock, feeling soft lips on mine, and all I could think was what do I do with my hands? Run your fingers through his hair, I thought, remembering Nesta's advice. I reached up to the back of his head but my fingers got stuck. Gel. His hair was like glue. Oh no. And I still had my gum in my mouth. Gulp. I swallowed it.

Then I wondered what he'd done with his. He wasn't chewing any more.

Then I got an attack of the giggles.

'What are you laughing at?' he said, looking taken aback.

'Er, I just swallowed my gum.'

He looked at me mischievously. 'So did I.'

Then he did that staring at my mouth thing again and a thrill of anticipation ran through me. It's the strangest feeling in the world, like a sweet pain but just lovely.

'Come here,' he said, pulling me close to him again and putting my arms round his waist. Then he kissed me properly. A lovely soft, deep kiss and this time our noses didn't bang. It felt perfect. Cosmic. And I wanted it to go on for ever.

'You're a good kisser,' he said, pulling back after a few minutes.

'Thanks,' I said, thinking Yippee! I'm a natural! Then I kissed him again. Practise makes perfect. That's going to be my new motto.

We must have stood there for ages. About half a dozen buses came and went and we were still snuggled up to each other, snogging away.

'So we should do this again, huh?' Mark asked, as another bus arrived at the stop.

I nodded.

'Oi! You getting on or not?' called the bus driver as the doors opened.

'Better had,' I said to Mark, after checking my watch.

'I'll call you, then, Izzie Foster,' he grinned, and off he went.

# COSMIC KISSES
## by Izzie Foster

I'm sending you cosmic kisses straight from my heart;
A planet collision won't tear us apart.
The distance between us is never too far;
I'll hitch a ride on a comet to get where you are.

In a moment a glance became a kiss,
In a heartbeat I knew my world had changed
For better, forever there is no other.
You're one in a million, of that I'm sure,
One in a million and I'm feeling so secure.

Cos I'm sending you cosmic kisses straight from my heart;
A planet collision won't tear us apart.
The distance between us is never too far;
I'll hitch a ride on a comet to get where you are.

# Chapter 11

# What Fresh Hell is This?

Last week of term. Teachers are relaxed, school is decorated for Christmas, with a huge tree in the hall, and generally everyone's in a good mood.

Except me. I'm Scrooge. Bah. Humbug. Pooh.

For our last English class, Mr Johnson asked us all to take in our favourite book of the year and pick out a quote from it to read to the class.

Half the class brought in the Harry Potters, a few brought in one of Philip Pullman's trilogy and Mary O'Connor brought a book called *Angus, Thongs and Full-frontal Snogging* by someone called Louise Rennison. It's the confessions of a fourteen-year-old girl and it made everyone laugh (even me, despite my current mood) when Mary read out a section. I took my book by Dorothy Parker as I'd read all of it now.

'Izzie, let's hear your quote,' said Mr Johnson.

'It's only a short one,' I said. 'By Dorothy Parker.'

Mr Johnson raised an eyebrow. 'Fine. Short is good,' he said. 'Go ahead.'

'What fresh hell is this?' I read from my book.

Mr Johnson looked taken aback. 'Why did you choose that, Izzie?'

'Seemed appropriate,' I said.

Mr Johnson creased up laughing. 'Trust you to be different, Izzie.'

It really did seem appropriate. Just as things were going swimmingly and I thought I was Snog Queen of North London, I'm into a whole new layer of torture in the boy/girl thing. Mark said he'd phone. And I was *so* sure he would this time. Positive. I mean, after all that fab snogging, how could he resist?

But he did. Resist, that is.

I'd wanted to phone him the minute I got home from our date just to hear his voice but when I reported back to Nesta and Lucy, both of them said I mustn't. I have to give him space.

'But I have his number now,' I said.

'I spoke to Tony about it,' said Nesta, 'and he agrees. Let Mark phone you.'

Tony? She'd been discussing me with Tony?

'But surely now, now that we've *snogged* and everything.

Surely it would be OK to get in touch?' I said to Lucy on my next call.

'Not really,' she said. 'I've been reading all about it in my *Men Are From Mars, Women Are From Venus* book. It says men fear intimacy and you mustn't pressurise them or they run away into a cave or somewhere. You have to pretend that they're like a rubber band. Let them expand as far as they want, then thwang, they come back to you. Nesta agrees with me. Don't call him.'

I couldn't *believe* it. Everyone's been discussing me. They've probably posted a site on the internet: www. whatdoyouthinkIzzieshoulddonext.com.

My *private* business.

What. Fresh. Hell. Is. This?

As the days went by and no call came, the temptation of having his home number was too much to resist.

One night, I rang his number (but not before dialling 141 first, so he wouldn't know it was me, I'm not *that* stupid) but all I got was an answering machine. I put the phone down quick.

The next night, I phoned again but chickened out before anyone picked up. Maybe Lucy and Nesta were right. I must be patient.

Patient. Patient. Patient. Not.

I rang again the next night. This time he picked up.

I panicked when I heard his voice and slammed the phone down. He was there. He *could* have phoned me. What was he doing that was more important?

Maybe I'd said something that had annoyed him. I went over every bit of our conversation in my head, trying to see what it might have been. Was it because I'd caught him out about his mobile phone? What was it? Didn't he fancy me any more? Or was it because now we'd snogged, he'd made the conquest and there was no more challenge?

Maybe, *oh no*, maybe he's met someone else.

The next night, I planned exactly what I was going to say. Bright, breezy, casual.

I got the answering machine again.

'Er, hi . . .' I said. 'It's me. Just wondering what's happening.'

I put the phone down. Just wondering what's happening? What's *that* supposed to mean? Happening as in on the planet? Or he might think I'm doing a heavy, like what's happening with *us*? I didn't mean it like *that*. It was meant to be cool, like durrh, what's happening, dude? He'll think I'm a dork. Then I remembered I'd said, 'It's me.' He might wonder who me is.

I called again.

'In case you're wondering who me is. It's me, Izzie.'

Oh pants. My brilliant speech had gone. I put the phone down. Now he'd definitely think I'm desperate. Too eager. Oh why didn't he call me? What's *wrong* with me?

In RE on Friday, we had poor Miss Hartley again. It was our last day before the Christmas break and everyone was in a giddier mood than usual.

By now, I think she'd had enough of us and had come up with a way of making us shut up. Or so she thought.

'OK, class, as we've been taking a look at religions and God over the last few weeks, I thought we'd do some-thing practical for a change. We're going to look at prayer and meditation.'

Brill, I thought. Just what I need. Something to still my mind and all the voices in my head driving me mad. Phone. Don't phone. Phone. Don't phone.

'First you have twenty minutes to write a prayer,' she said. 'Don't worry, we won't be reading them out loud. They're just for you.'

Good, I thought. I have a few things I want to say to God. I got out my paper and started writing.


*Dear God*

*I know you're busy doing a million things, spinning planets, keeping it all in balance and all, but please could you spare me a moment?*

*But then, you're omniscient, so you probably know what I'm going to say anyway. So maybe I shouldn't waste your time.*

*But then again you live in eternity, so you have all the time in the world. God, it's confusing.*

*Anyway. Could you . . .? Of course you could, you're omnipotent as well. Maybe I shouldn't ask for anything. You know best really. Maybe you should let me know what to pray for because sometimes I don't know.*

*PS Please could you make Mark phone me or else stop me feeling as mad as I do lately.*

*PPS Please could my bum stop growing now. I think it's big enough.*

*PPS Let there be peace and everybody be happy with no wars.*

*That is if that's all OK with you and doesn't interfere with your plans. Amen.*

*With love, Izzie Foster*

After twenty minutes, Miss Hartley started up again.

'See, we are called human beings,' she said, 'but when do we ever *be*? We're always human *doings*, dashing about doing this and that. We never stop to just be.'

I liked the sound of that. To be a human *being*. Cool.

'Anyway, as prayer is talking to God,' she continued, 'so meditation is listening. The idea is to find a quiet place within yourself and let the silence speak to you. Try to imagine that your mind is like the sea. On the surface are all the waves of thoughts, up and down they go. But if you go deep, deep, fathom deep into the sea, you'll find stillness no matter what's happening on the surface. It's the same with our minds – thoughts, feelings, all bounce about on the top, but if you go deeper, then there's stillness.'

Perfect, I thought. It's a shame everyone gave Miss Hartley such a hard time. She talked a lot of sense to me. I couldn't wait to try it.

'Now different methods work for different people,' said Miss Hartley. 'I want you all to make yourselves comfortable and then close your eyes and focus inside. Some people find it helps to have something to concentrate on, like a mantra. Does anyone know what that is?'

I put up my hand. 'It's a word, miss.'

'That's right, Izzie, a popular one is "Om". What you do is think about the word "Om" and say it over and over again, silently in your head. Right, let's begin. Eyes closed. Let your mind go still. Meditate.'

I did as I was told and tried to make my mind go blank.

Thought 1: My mind is blank.

Thought 2: It can't be. You just thought that thought.

Thought 3: What thought?

Thought 4: The one about being blank. If you were really blank, you wouldn't think anything.

Thought 5: OK. Try again.

Thought 6: I could kill Nesta for telling Tony my business.

Thought 7: Why oh *why* hasn't Mark phoned?

Thought 8: I've been an *idiot*. I shouldn't have called him.

Thought 9: But why *can't* a girl phone a boy?

Thought 10: This isn't helping at all. OK. Be quiet again. Try the mantra. Om. Om. Om. Om. Om. Oh pooh. Pooh. Pooh. Got an itch.

Thought 11: How many people are there in my head? I think I may be going mad. Om, om, ommmmmmmm.

Thought 12: I think I'll just have a peek to see how Lucy and Nesta are getting on.

I opened one eye and had a quick look around the room.

Most people were sitting quietly with their eyes shut. Candice Carter looked as though she was asleep as she was nodding forward and any minute now her head would crash into her desk.

I glanced over at Lucy. She had one eye open as well. Our eyes met and we giggled.

Then someone started at the back of the class.

'Kneedeep.' A frog sound.

'Tweet twoo.' Someone did an owl sound.

'Meeow.' I did a cat.

'Mooooo.' That was Lucy.

The whole class joined in with animal sounds until it sounded like a farmyard.

'Girls, *girls*!' cried Miss Hartley. 'What on earth do you think you're doing?'

By now, we were all laughing our heads off.

So much for Christmas meaning goodwill to all men and schoolgirls. We all got detention and had to stay in at lunch-time. *Detention.* On the last day of term? Bah. Humbug. But I was feeling marginally better. Perhaps prayer and meditation do work after all.

Then maybe so does a good laugh.

In detention, Miss Hartley gave us instructions to write out hymns.

'Now I'm going next door to the staffroom,' she said. 'And if anyone speaks, there'll be another fifteen minutes' detention.'

We all did a few lines, then I got bored so I wrote a song about boys not phoning. Then I had an idea. Miss Hartley said if anyone speaks we'd get another fifteen minutes. She didn't say anything about singing.

It is Christmas after all. I started up a hymn and soon everyone joined in.

*'We Three Kings of Orient are,*
*One in a taxi, one in a car,*
*One on his scooter,*
*Tooting his hooter,*
*Following yonder star.'*

At last, term was over. A Merry Christmas one and all.

# CUT THE CONNECTION
## by Izzie Foster

You think you're going out tonight, but you'll be
    staying in,
You'll sigh, you'll cry, you'll wonder why the phone will
    never ring.

You know he's playing games like every other boy,
But you don't care though you're aware he treats you
    like a toy.

He says he'll be there for you when all the chips are down,
But he's said the same to every girl in town.

He doesn't care you're in despair as tears burn in your
    eyes.
You'll sigh, you'll cry, you'll wonder why all he says is lies.

Cut the connection, turn off the phone, grab hold of life
    and you won't be alone.
Believe in yourself and no one else and you'll find that
    you have grown.
So cut the connection, turn off the phone, grab hold of
    life and you won't be alone.

# Chapter 12

# Happy
## Eater

The next morning, Mum was up early and decorating our Christmas tree in her usual immaculate manner. White and silver, each bauble placed with precision and each necklace of tinsel making a perfect circle round the branches. What a contrast to the tree at Lucy's, I thought. Theirs looks like someone got out a box of coloured balls and tinsel and threw it at the tree. Mum's does look nice though, elegant, very *Homes and Gardens*.

'Want to help?' asked Mum.

'Not really,' I said, flopping on one of the sofas. I knew from past experience there wasn't much point. She had it very clear in her head what she wanted it to look like and I'd be bound to put a star or something in the wrong place.

'What's up, Izzie?' asked Mum, putting down the tinsel and sitting on the sofa opposite me.

'Nothing,' I said.

'Oh, that again,' she smiled. 'Nothing always gets me down as well.'

'It's just, I dunno, end of term and everything . . .'

'You're usually ecstatic at the end of term.'

'Yeah, but you know, I dunno . . .'

Mum sat, looking at me with concern. 'I do wish you'd talk to me, Izzie. Perhaps I can help.'

No chance, I thought. No one can help.
'I just feel I think one thing then go and do another. Like I've been trying to eat healthily then I decided I could have the odd treat. Then found I was having *loads* of treats and only the odd healthy thing. I can't even get that right. I'm hopeless.'

'You're only human, Iz,' said Mum. 'But it's not just that, is it?'

I shrugged.

'Is it that boy who called?' Mum asked.

'Who *didn't* call, you mean,' I said. 'And I don't know what I've done wrong.'

'Probably nothing. Boys can be strange creatures. Call when you don't expect but never when you do.'

'Tell me about it,' I said. 'There should be classes in all that *Men Are From Mars, Women Are From Venus* stuff. You know, we do all these classes in school but none of it really helps. Not with real life.'

'I know,' said Mum. 'I remember when I was your age, or perhaps a little older, and just getting interested in boys. All the Latin, Maths and Literature wasn't much use when I had a crush on someone.'

'That's just it. No one teaches you how to handle it. What to do if he phones, or doesn't? I seem to have got it all wrong.'

Mum smiled. 'Our school wasn't much help either. It was a very strict convent school. At least you get some sex education these days. I remember when I was about sixteen, we were all called into see the Mother Superior who explained about periods. "It happens to everyone, even the Virgin Mary," she said, as if that was supposed to make us feel better. Bit late, we all thought – some girls had started years earlier.'

I smiled. It was hard to imagine my mum as an innocent teenager, she always seemed so sure of herself.

'And another time,' Mum continued, 'we had to go and see Mother Superior again. This time it was handy hints for parties. "If you're at a party," she said, "and the lights go out, stand in a corner and shout at the top of your voice, I'm a Catholic!" '

'How was that supposed to help?' I laughed.

'Exactly,' said Mum. 'Convent girls had a bit of a reputation back then so we all thought it was hilarious. Like every boy in the room would think, Right lads, the convent girls are in the corner. And then she told us that it was permissible to sit on a boy's knee but only if a book the thickness of a telephone directory was put on his lap.'

By now, I had the giggles. 'Poor you,' I said.

At that moment, the doorbell rang. 'I'll get that,' grinned Mum.

She was back a few moments later with what looked like a large box of groceries.

All the yummy Christmas food, I thought to myself. How will I ever resist?

'Come into the kitchen,' said Mum.

I followed her in, hoping she wasn't going to give me a lecture on eating what I was given.

'Ta-da!' said Mum with a flourish as she pulled out a pizza box. 'Look what I've got.'

What had come over her? She was acting really strange.

'Look,' she beamed. 'Organic pizza.' She carried on pulling out a range of goodies from the box. 'Muesli, you like that, don't you? Free-range eggs. Brown rice. Wholemeal bread. Mince pies *without* beef suet. Ingredients for a nut roast for Christmas day. But best of all, ice cream made with organic chocolate, no added preservatives. Get a spoon. Let's try it.'

I looked in the box. She'd bought loads of fresh fruit and vegetables as well. 'Mum, this is amazing!'

'I know. I never knew there was such a fantastic range of organic food around now. See in my day, healthy meant tasteless. Boring. But all the shops sell organic now. And it looks great. And after my little talk with Mr Lovering . . .'

'Ah . . . So that's what it was about?'

Mum nodded and sat down at the kitchen table. 'I've been so worried about you, Izzie, and your strange eating fads. Mr Lovering gave me a few tips. And it's probably about time I changed my eating habits too. You were right. I do tend to eat on the go and grab whatever's to hand. From now on, we eat healthy in this house.'

I went over to her and gave her a huge hug. 'Thanks, Mum.'

'No problem,' she smiled and hugged me back. 'Between us, we'll find a balance we're *both* happy with. We have fresh and healthy with our fruit and veg. But we can still have our treats.'

'Great,' I said. 'So where's that organic ice cream you mentioned?'

# Chapter 13

# Sleepover Secrets

Later that day, I went over to Nesta's. We were having a sleepover and were going to decide what to wear for the prom the next night.

I hadn't told them yet that I'd decided not to go.

Lucy was already there when I arrived. She was looking gorgeous in a short black skirt and a lilac crop top that she'd made. Plus she was wearing eye make-up *and* lippie. A lot of effort for a night in, I thought, but of course to Lucy it was more than that. It was a sleepover in the same house as her boyfriend. Mmm. Should be interesting.

Nesta's mum and dad were going to a concert somewhere in town and popped in to say goodnight before they left.

'There's plenty of clean bedding in the spare room for you and Lucy,' said Mrs Williams. 'Anything you need Nesta will find for you.'

'Thanks, Mrs Williams,' I said.

She looked great, all dressed up for the evening in a black velvet top and trousers. She's very glamorous is Nesta's mum.

'Don't stay up too late,' said Mr Williams, coming in behind her. He's Italian and very handsome, like a movie star. With parents as good-looking as they are, it's no wonder Nesta's such a stunner.

When they'd gone, Nesta brought up the important business of choosing our outfits.

'Fashion show, fashion show,' said Nesta. 'Mum got me a new dress. I can't wait to show you.'

She disappeared for a few minutes then came back wearing a short silky silver dress with sequins round the neck. She looked fantastic, legs right up to her armpits, lucky thing.

'You look gorgeous,' I said. 'Shoes?'

'Dunno,' said Nesta, holding up two pairs. 'Black and strappy or these silver ones? Do you think they're a bit summery?'

'No, perfect for the dress,' said Lucy. 'Anyway, it'll be boiling once we start dancing. What about you, Iz? What are you going to wear?'

'Not going,' I said.

Nesta and Lucy looked appalled.

'What do mean, not going?' said Nesta.

I shrugged. 'Not in the mood.'

'But I thought Mark said he was going?' said Lucy.

'He did. But he hasn't phoned to ask if we can go together and I don't want to bump into him and go through all that stuff again. I realised that I've been doing all the running. No, if he wants to see me, he can make an effort.'

'Quite right,' said Nesta. 'But I don't see why you should miss the prom because of him.'

'You've got to come, Iz,' said Lucy. 'I thought you wanted to see King Noz play. You can ignore Mark if he's there. And we'll be there. Me and Nesta.'

I wasn't convinced. 'Anyway, I've got nothing to wear. What are you wearing, Lucy?'

'I made something specially,' she said. Lucy is a real whiz on the sewing machine. She's made me and Nesta tops in the past and they're really fantastic, professional- looking. 'You'll see tomorrow – it's a surprise.'

'Please come, Izzie,' begged Nesta. 'It won't be the same without you and remember what we said about not letting a boy come between us.'

I did remember. And she was right. I was letting it all get to me again. Running around, trying to bump into him accidentally-on-purpose hadn't worked. Neither had all that waiting in for the phone. Maybe cutting off and hiding away wouldn't work either? Oh why couldn't it be simple? Then I thought, why *should* I let Mark ruin my Christmas? So he didn't phone. I'd had enough of letting him affect my moods.

'I suppose I could come for an hour or so,' I said.

'Fantastic,' said Lucy, then grinned mysteriously. 'Anyway, I brought something for us to try tonight. Just up your street, Izzie, to get you in the party mood.'

Half an hour later I found myself standing in front of the mirror in Nesta's bedroom while she and Lucy coached me from Nesta's bed.

'Again,' demanded Lucy. 'Again, but try to make it more convincing. Try and *feel* the words.'

The mystery 'something' was one of her mum's self- help books on affirmations.

'Just what you need,' said Lucy before we got started. 'You say the affirmations over and over again until your mind starts to believe what you're saying and it becomes real for you.'

She and Nesta had pored through the book until finally they picked one for me.

'Say it again,' said Lucy.

I straightened my shoulders. 'I *am* full of joy,' I intoned to the gloomy face looking back out at me. 'I am full of joy.'

Nesta shook her head. 'Yeah, looks like it.'

I slumped back on to the bed next to her. 'Sorry, girls, I did try.'

'Maybe it's not the right affirmation for you,' said Lucy, going back to her book. It was called *Change Your Life by Changing Your Thoughts*.

'OK, read me some of the others,' I said. I knew she

was trying to be helpful. The least I could do was go along with it.

'*I'm light, I'm bright, I've got it right.* Nah, that's not appropriate.' She flicked the pages.

'Try another,' said Nesta.

'*I'm slim and healthy, successful and wealthy,*' read Lucy.

'You do that one, Nesta,' I said.

Nesta stood up and went to the mirror. 'I'm slim and healthy, successful and wealthy. I'm slim and healthy, successful and wealthy. Is there one for what to do with big feet?'

I found a new page. 'How about this one? *To find repose I relax to my toes.* No? OK. Pooh to that. Try *I am feeling warm and mild, cradling my inner child.*'

'Oh yerghhhh. No thanks,' cried Nesta. 'Vomitous!'

'No, no, don't give up,' I said, getting into it. 'Oh, here's one for me. Perfect, in the self-esteem section. *I am a perfect size, I have beautiful thighs.* Or Everyone knows, *I love my nose.*'

Nesta and I cracked up laughing.

Lucy grabbed the book from me and flicked through the pages again. 'How do you expect to change your lives when you keep laughing? Here, try this, Iz: *I affirm that now I can, attract the perfect man.* Come on, stand up and say it to your reflection.'

'Do I have to?'

'Yes.'

I stood up. 'I affirm that now I can, attract the perfect

man. I affirm that now I can, attract the perfect man. I affirm that now I can, attract the perfect man.'

At that moment, Tony walked in.

'And here I am,' he grinned, then went over to Lucy and gave her a peck on the cheek. 'Coming into my room, Luce?'

Lucy went bright red like she always does when Tony's around, then stood up and meekly followed him out of the room.

'Hmmm,' I said. 'Should be interesting.'

'He'd better not try anything,' said Nesta. 'Or I'll kill him.'


Nesta and I spent the rest of the evening doing our nails and trying out make-up. Nesta painted her nails her usual dark purple and I did mine blue then put a layer of glitter on top.

'I affirm that now I can, attract the perfect man,' we said over and over as we waited for our nails to dry. Then we did the affirmations again in all the accents we knew. Scottish, American, Indian, Irish, Cockney.

After that, Nesta showed me a dance routine that she'd worked out for the prom tomorrow. Not to be outdone, I showed her a routine I used to do in Irish dancing when I was at junior school.

We collapsed on the sofa after fifteen minutes of mad Irish dancing and watched Nesta's DVD collection of *How I Met Your Mother* and soon it was half past eleven. There was still no sign of Lucy or Tony.

Nesta made up beds for me and Lucy in their spare room then went and banged on Tony's door. It was locked.

'Bed-time, Lucy. What are you doing in there?'

We heard stifled giggles then Tony's voice. 'Nothing,' he said.

'Well me and Izzie are going to bed and you'd better be out of there before Mum and Dad get home,' said Nesta.

More stifled giggles.

'I hope she's all right in there,' said Nesta, looking concerned.

'So do I,' I said, then knocked again. 'Lucy. *Lucy*. Sure you're OK?'

'Yeah, fine,' called Lucy. 'Be out in a minute.'

'Or two,' said Tony.


I settled down in my bed in the spare room and snuggled in to go to sleep. What a few weeks, I thought. At least things are better with Mum now. We had a really good time this morning and it reminded me she can be OK sometimes. And I suppose I have been a bit of a pain lately. Not my fault totally though, as Pluto *has* been going through an intense phase in my horoscope and it made everything seem complicated. I still think there's something to astrology no matter what Lucy thinks. But I'll make it my New Year's resolution not to be so obsessive. And to be nicer to Mum. And I'll even try being nicer to Angus. He was really cool about the wedding photos the other night. It was his daughter's wedding album I'd supposedly ruined but he'd made it OK in the end.

As I went through my list of resolutions I started to nod off.

I was almost asleep when I heard the door open and Lucy crept in. I switched the light on and looked at my watch. It was past twelve.

'Sorry, did I wake you?' said Lucy.

'S'OK,' I said sleepily, 'You OK?'

Lucy sat on her bed and sighed. 'Not really.'

'What is it?' I said, sitting up. She looked close to tears.

'Promise you won't tell Nesta?'

'Promise,' I said.

'Because if you do, she's bound to have a go at Tony and then he really will dump me.'

'Why, what's he done?'

Lucy hesitated. 'Wandering hands,' she said finally.

'Oh.'

'I don't know what to do, Iz. I'm happy just kissing. But he always wants to take it further. And I don't. I'm just not ready. He says it's because I'm too young for him and he knew this would happen. He says maybe it's best we don't see each other and then he can go out with someone more his own age.'

'Oh Lucy . . . ' I began.

'What he means is someone who won't say no to him. So what do I do? If I don't play along, I'll lose him and he's the first boy I've ever really liked. But if I do play along, who knows what will happen? Maybe he'll dump me anyway. Nesta's always said he loses interest when there's no challenge left.'

'It's not fair,' I said, suddenly feeling angry about Tony and about Mark. 'Why should boys always be the ones who call the shots? It should be us. Tony's acting like a spoiled kid who can't have what he wants, and threatening you. Don't let him get away with it, Luce.'

'You think?'

'Yeah. Take control. Dump *him*. He's making you feel bad. Tell him *you* think it's not working out and you'll see how you feel about it all later but right now, you're not ready. You should feel you can trust Tony and you obviously don't. It should feel really special. You should be the one that chooses. You shouldn't feel forced into anything you don't want to do.'

'Maybe we should see what my horoscope says about it,' said Lucy.

'I thought you said you didn't believe in astrology,' I said.

'I never,' said Lucy. 'I just thought you were taking it all too seriously, that's all.'

'Well, I've realised a lot about all that in the last few weeks. Astrology can give you *some* clues as to what's happening but you were right, you can't let it rule your life. It's what you make of it all in the end. You have to take control, make things happen or not. Choose.'

'Even if I lose Tony?' said Lucy sadly.

'What are you losing?' I said, growing more and more sure as I spoke. 'We have each other. You, me and Nesta. We should be the ones that choose or else we're all going to go through hell, up and down and round and round, trying to please boys but losing ourselves in the process.'

I was only too aware that all I was saying applied to me as well as Lucy.

Lucy smiled weakly. 'I suppose you're right. Boys, huh? Can't live with them, can't live without them.'

'No, *can* live with them, *can* live without them. From now on, we call the shots.'

# DAMAGED BEAUTY
## by Izzie Foster

He's frequently flawless but often unkind,
This fallen angel drives you out of your mind.
He's the devil beneath you and you ought to know,
He has to go, you really should know.

The gift you are given is kindness and grace
But each time you fall for a handsome young face.
Stop looking for light in love's gloomy rooms,
Throw open the windows
Let in the sun, you're number one.

Look into your heart, just make a start.
You really know, he has to go.

Put your damaged beauty in a silent place,
There's new love just waiting, get back in the race.
Shout out you're ready, cast into the pool,
This time remember, don't land a fool.

Look into your heart, make a brand new start.
Look into your heart, it's up to you.

# Chapter 14

# Girl
## Power

**Mum** dropped me off at the prom at about eight thirty the following night and already the place was buzzing with a party atmosphere. People were up and dancing, Lady Gaga was blaring out through large speakers on either side of the hall, and Mrs Allen and Mr Johnson, wearing daft Santa hats, were standing by the drinks table. Probably on the look-out for boys adding vodka like they did last year. Half the school was out of their skulls by midnight and the other half sick all over the place. It was a riot when parents arrived to pick people up, with the teachers getting the tellings off for a change.

I had a quick glance round the hall before taking my coat to the cloakroom. The place was unrecognisable as the usual hall where we had assembly. The Christmas tree had been moved up on to the stage where equipment had been set up for the band, and fairy lights were strung all along the walls.

I put my coat away then went into a cubicle to change. I'd been over to see Dad and Anna this morning and was having a moan about having nothing to wear for the prom.

'Well, I was going to give you this for Christmas, but if you really want, you could have it now,' said Dad. 'Probably best you pick something you want yourself.'

Then he handed me a fifty-pound note.

I gave him a huge hug then dashed out to Primrose Hill. The black velvet dress I'd seen weeks ago was still in the window and had been reduced in a Christmas sale. It fitted perfectly, really tight and made me look tall and slim. I was a bit worried Mum wouldn't let me wear it tonight as it's backless and a bit low at the front, but she agreed on condition I wore a little top underneath. Which of course I did.

In the cubicle, I took off the little top and put it in my bag, then I put on a heart pendant I'd borrowed from Mum's jewellery box. I went and checked my appearance in the mirror and applied a bit of red lippie then made my way into the main hall and soon found Nesta.

'This place is poser's heaven,' I said, looking at all our class swanning about in their posh party frocks.

'I know,' said Nesta. 'Great, isn't it? Hey, you look gorgeous. Great dress. Really sophisticated.'

'Thanks,' I said. 'So do you.'

Nesta looked beautiful in her sparkly silver dress and her hair like black silk right down to her waist. She'd soon get off with someone and Lucy, of course, would be with Tony. I hoped I wasn't going to be the only one on my own.

'Have you seen Jade Wilcocks?' said Nesta. 'She's got a ton of make-up on. I saw her just now in the corridor, all over some boy.'

'She's not the only one. On the way from the cloakroom, I saw half a dozen couples having snogathons.'

'It's going to be a good party,' grinned Nesta. 'What time's the band on?'

'Soon I think,' I said, looking at my watch. 'Where's Lucy?'

'Putting some silver shimmer through her hair in the cloakroom,' she said. 'She looks amazing. And you know she's dumped Tony?'

'You're kidding. When?'

'This morning after you'd gone.'

'Is she OK?'

'Yeah,' said Nesta. 'She's fine. Great. It's hysterical. It's Tony who's not. He couldn't believe it even though she did it really nicely. She spent ages talking to him. But he's never been dumped before. He's always been the dumper. He's gone into shock, I think. He was lolling about all morning, saying Lucy was special, not like other girls. He's phoned her about ten times today.'

'Hiya,' said Lucy, coming to join us.

'Wow,' I said. 'You look fab. Like a Christmas fairy.'

Lucy had a short white backless dress on with delicate sparkling straps and a silver hem. Her hair was subtly glittering.

'Did you make that dress?' I asked.

Lucy nodded. 'Like it? I made it last week. I read in a mag that if you show off your back no one will notice you haven't got any boobs.'

I laughed. Having a flat chest was Lucy's big hang-up but she needn't worry. She looked fantastic.

'It looks great,' said Nesta.

'But tell me about Tony,' I said. 'What happened?'

Lucy grinned. 'It didn't feel right any more.'

I couldn't believe it. She was being so cool.

'But you really liked him!'

'I know, but after last night, I realised you were right. I was getting more and more miserable trying to be and do what he wanted. I want it to feel really special and I'm just not sure of him yet. Anyway, it *should* be us girls that call the shots. And I decided I just wasn't ready.' She looked anxiously at Nesta, but she was busy giving some boy the eye. 'After last night, I thought I don't want to be poor little Lucy. Dumped because she's too young. I decided to turn the tables.'

'Good for you, Luce,' I said. 'I think you're really brave.

And looking like this, you'll get off with someone else really easily.'

Just at that moment, the lights went down and a hush fell over the hall. I looked up at the stage and saw a boy go over to the main mike and pick up a guitar.

He looked familiar. Oh no. It was Ben. Oh *no*, I thought, he's going to play more of his appalling songs from the shows. He'll look a right prat in front of this lot. He must be the warm-up act to King Noz. I wondered what idiot booked him.

At that moment, he looked down and caught my eye and gave me a wave. I waved back nervously. Oh dear. Now everyone would know that I know him and it's going to be so embarrassing when he starts playing.

'And now,' said the DJ. 'Let's hear a big round of applause for King Noz.'

*What*? I thought. It *can't* be.

Three other boys walked out on the stage to join Ben and took their places, one at the keyboards, and the other two on guitar. Then they started playing and Ben started singing. He was amazing. *They* were amazing. Totally amazing. Everyone went mad, clapping and cheering then manic dancing in time to the music.

My jaw must have dropped open because Lucy turned to me.

'What's the matter, Iz?'

'I *know* him,' I stuttered. 'That's Ben up there.'

'I know. He comes to Dad for lessons. He's brilliant, isn't he?'

'But he's the guy from the wedding . . . ' I said. I couldn't get my head round it. The same Ben that had looked so awkward playing at the wedding was now up on stage giving it all he'd got and looking mucho cute. Everyone was up on their feet, dancing away. The audience loved them.

After a couple of fast numbers, Ben took the mike. 'And now we're going to slow it down a bit,' he said. He swapped places with the keyboard player and they began to play again.

Girls paired off with boys to slow dance as Ben sang a lovely ballad. He was really good. A strong clear voice. I couldn't believe I'd been such a nerd. I should have realised. But how was I to know that *he* was King Noz?

As the band upped the pace again Nesta disappeared into the throng with some boy who'd asked her to dance. I watched her doing the routine she'd shown me the night before. Everyone was watching her but some of the girls didn't seem too happy about the way their boyfriends were ogling.

Lucy put her hand on my arm. 'Don't look now. Mark's just arrived.'

I quickly turned away but too late, he'd seen me and was walking towards me, smiling.

'Izzie,' he said, putting his arm round me. 'You look

fantastic. I was hoping you'd be here. Wanna dance?'

I couldn't believe his cheek. Hoping I'd be there. Why didn't he phone and make sure?

'No thanks,' I said. 'I want to listen to the band.'

He looked taken aback. Actually I did want to listen to the band but I also wasn't going to fall into his arms the minute he arrived.

'Maybe later,' I said.

'Oh, OK,' he said. 'I'll go and get a drink, then. Want anything?'

'No thanks,' I said, turning back to the stage as he walked off looking puzzled.

'Good for you, Iz,' said Lucy.

I took a deep breath. I wasn't feeling as confident as I may have looked. Mark was still cute but I had made a promise to myself that I wasn't going to be such a pushover in future.

'Anyway, I think Ben likes you,' said Lucy, pointing at the stage.

I turned to look at him and sure enough, he was looking at me as he sang the words of a song.

'Do you think?'

'I do,' said Lucy. 'He's really nice, you know. I've talked to him when he's been waiting for lessons at home sometimes. He thinks about stuff like you do. I reckon you'd get on.'

I spent the next half-hour standing by the wall, listening to the set King Noz played.

'*There's a secret there for learning,*' Ben sang. '*A journey to be taken in my search for truth. Krishna, Buddha, Gandhi, Christ, all bid me follow but which road offers proof? While I seek the smiles of angels, darkness calls my soul, Jesus help me fight the fight, Buddha lead me to the light.*'

Then he went into a rap chorus, '*Omnipresent, omni-where? I look for God but is he there? Heaven, hell, a state of mind. The way is lost for our mankind.*'

As I listened to the lyrics I thought, Lucy's right, I would get on with Ben. He seems to be asking all the same questions as me. Even if we didn't get off with each other, we obviously had a lot we could talk about. I'd never even given him a second glance. Not considered him for a moment. But watching him up there playing, I had to admit I was impressed. Very impressed.

When the band had finished playing, the DJ started up the prom again and I could see Ben heading towards me.

'You were fantastic,' I said. 'Really brilliant.'

He looked pleased. 'Thanks. Bit of a change from songs from the shows.'

'A bit,' I smiled, thinking he had really nice blue eyes with thick black lashes behind his little round glasses.

'My brother made me get up at that wedding. I felt a right prat. But it was his wedding and that's what he wanted.'

'Right,' I said, not wanting to admit that I'd put him in a box and labelled it naff.

'Have you been playing long?' I asked.

'About four years. Lot to learn still, that's why I'm taking lessons. In fact, there was something I wanted to ask you about.'

Suddenly he looked embarrassed.

'What?' I asked.

'Well, I know I shouldn't have looked and I know I should have asked . . . '

'What are you on about?' I asked.

'Well, you know that day I saw you at Lucy's house? When I was there for my lesson?'

'Yeah?'

'Well, after the lesson Mr Lovering went off to find some CDs for me and I was just sat there waiting . . . '

'And?'

'And I saw this book on the piano. It had your name on it.'

'Oh no,' I said. 'Oh *no*. You didn't look, did you?'

He nodded, 'I did. I didn't mean to . . . '

'I never show anybody my lyrics, not *anybody*.' I felt awful. He'd laugh at me just as I've decided I like him. And his songs are so good, he must think mine are awful.

'I'm sorry,' he continued. 'As I said, I didn't mean to look, not for long, but I really liked what I read. Did you write all those songs yourself?'

I nodded.

'They're really good, Izzie. In fact, I wanted to ask

you . . . Have you put any of them to music yet?'

I shook my head.

'Well, what do you think about us getting together sometime and working on them?'

'Honestly?' I asked. I couldn't think of anything I'd like better.

We spent the next half-hour talking about bands we liked and who we didn't, when we were interrupted by Mark.

'Dance?' he said, giving Ben a filthy look.

I was feeling so pleased with the way everything was turning out, I accepted. As I danced with Mark I could see Ben watching me.

Mmm, I thought. Could be interesting.

'So,' said Mark. 'Want to go out next week?'

I shrugged. 'Maybe. I don't know what I'm doing yet.'

Again, he looked totally taken aback. 'Oh well, phone me when you do,' he said.

'Yeah,' I said, enjoying the effect I was having on him.

He leaned close to me and whispered, 'Because I really like you, Izzie.'

'Yeah,' I said. 'Whatever.'

He looked completely bemused. It was hysterical.

'Anyway, maybe catch you later,' I said. 'Got to go. I came with my friends. Got to find them.'

I left him standing in the middle of the dance floor with his mouth hanging open. That'll teach you, I thought. You could have come with me, *if* you'd bothered to phone.

The rest of the prom was brilliant. Nesta, in her usual style of fancying older boys, got off with some Sixth Former and was last seen in the canteen snogging for Britain.

Then Tony turned up.

'I have to speak to you,' he said urgently. 'About Lucy.'

'What about Lucy?' I asked, doing my best innocent face.

'Tell me what to do. You're one of her best mates. How can I get her back?'

'What does Nesta say?'

Tony laughed. 'Nesta? Nesta's told me from the beginning to keep away from Lucy. But I don't want to. I *really* like her.'

'She's over there,' I said, pointing out Lucy to him. She was slow dancing with a good-looking boy who looked really keen.

Tony's face dropped. 'I've blown it, haven't I?'

'Maybe,' I said. 'Maybe not. You never know until you've tried.'

What an evening, I thought, as Tony went on to the dance floor to cut in on Lucy. Boys. Strange species. Don't want you when you want them and do want you when you're not interested. But I'm learning. Fast.

As the party started to wind down, I went to go and get my coat and Ben caught up with me.

'Izzie,' he said. 'Can I phone you? You know, about getting together to do some songs?'

I was about to give him my number when I stopped and laughed.

'What's so funny?' asked Ben.

'Nothing,' I said, getting out my pen. 'I'd love to do some songs with you. But you give me *your* number. *I'll* call you.'